BORDERLAND BLOODBATH

Fargo leaped to his feet and lunged forward, driving the Arkansas toothpick deep into his assailant's torso and giving it the "Spanish twist." The man emitted a high-pitched scream of pain and dropped to the ground like a sack of grain, flopping wildly for a few seconds until death closed his account. The leather-wrapped blackjack he had used to sap Fargo was still clutched in his right hand.

All this had taken only seconds. Scar Face started to bolt toward the nearby mouth of the alley, but one of Fargo's long legs managed to hook him and send him sprawling. With lightning speed Fargo pinned him facedown with a knee in his back.

He grabbed a handful of hair and jerked the downed man's head back far enough to slip the toothpick's razor-honed edge in front of his windpipe. . . .

THE

TRAILSMAN

#388

BORDERLAND BLOODBATH

by

Jon Sharpe

A SIGNET BOOK

SIGNET
Published by the Penguin Group
Penguin Group (USA) LLC, 375 Hudson Street,
New York, New York 10014

USA | Canada | UK | Ireland | Australia | New Zealand | India | South Africa | China
penguin.com
A Penguin Random House Company

First published by Signet, an imprint of New American Library,
a division of Penguin Group (USA) LLC

First Printing, February 2014

The first chapter of this book previously appeared in *Apache Vendetta*, the three
hundred eighty-seventh volume in this series.

Ⓟ REGISTERED TRADEMARK—MARCA REGISTRADA

ISBN 978-0-451-46648-8

Printed in the United States of America
10 9 8 7 6 5 4 3 2 1

The Trailsman

Beginnings . . . they bend the tree and they mark the man. Skye Fargo was born when he was eighteen. Terror was his midwife, vengeance his first cry. Killing spawned Skye Fargo, ruthless, cold-blooded murder. Out of the acrid smoke of gunpowder still hanging in the air, he rose, cried out a promise never forgotten.

The Trailsman they began to call him all across the West: searcher, scout, hunter, the man who could see where others only looked, his skills for hire but not his soul, the man who lived each day to the fullest, yet trailed each tomorrow. Skye Fargo, the Trailsman, the seeker who could take the wildness of a land and the wanting of a woman and make them his own.

Rio Grande borderland, 1860—where Skye Fargo witnesses an international land grab and ends up stalked by the most fearsome assassin on the frontier.

1

The Ovaro gave his low trouble whicker, jolting Skye Fargo out of an uneasy sleep.

In one fluid, continuous movement only a heartbeat after his eyes snapped open, Fargo rolled out of his blanket, rose to a low crouch, shucked his walnut-grip Colt from his holster and thumb-cocked it.

At first, as the last cobwebs of sleep cleared from his mind, all seemed calm enough. Cicadas gave off their metronomic, singsong rhythm; the nearby Rio Grande purled gently only ten yards away; a fat full moon had turned from the buttery color of early evening to the pale white that preceded dawn.

Then Fargo heard it: a man's authoritative voice snapping out an indistinct command from about fifty yards upriver.

The Ovaro snorted, not liking this mysterious human intrusion.

"Steady on, old campaigner," Fargo said in a low voice, placing a hand on the stallion's neck to calm him. "Whoever they are, they don't know we're here."

It was 1860, the middle of the blistering dog days in the American Southwest, and the man some called the Trailsman had just finished a three-month stint riding security for a merchant caravan between Santa Fe and Guadalajara, Mexico. He had collected his final pay earlier in El Paso and pitched camp for the night in this juniper thicket on the American side of the sleepy, muddy, meandering river Mexicans called Río Bravo del Norte, Americans Rio Grande.

Another voice rang out upriver and again Fargo couldn't make out the words. But for some inexplicable reason an ominous sense of foreboding prickled his scalp.

"You picked the wrong campsite, Fargo," he muttered.

It wasn't just these voices now. Earlier, when Fargo was cleaning and oiling his brass-framed Henry rifle, a lone rider had moved in close, forcing Fargo to kick dirt over his small fire.

Still, such a level of activity was hardly surprising along the U.S.-Mexico border. *Contrabandistas*, slave-trading Comancheros, whiskey peddlers and gunrunners operated with impunity in this area, and they naturally preferred the cloak of darkness. Whoever they were, Fargo figured it was none of his mix.

Again the commanding voice and this time Fargo thought he had heard the English words "shore it up."

He moved cautiously forward out of the thicket, unpleasantly aware once again of a vaguely foreboding premonition of danger. Despite the warm night his skin goose bumped, stiffening the hair on his forearms.

Something's wrong, Fargo, insisted an urgent inner voice. *Something's dead wrong. Don't you notice what it is?*

Fargo emerged silently from the thicket and saw the river reflecting glimmering points of color in the moonlight despite being at its muddiest by late summer. He glanced upriver and spotted torches burning. But he couldn't see much because the black velvet folds of darkness seemed to absorb the illumination before it reached his eyes.

More words reached him now, muffled by the distance and the constant chuckling of the river: ". . . Use plenty . . . not too deep . . . more past the bend . . ."

Occasionally he spotted ghostly figures moving in and out of the light. He listened carefully to a steady chunking sound and recognized it as several shovels digging. Men burying contraband, maybe, but why so close to the water?

What's wrong, Fargo? that insistent inner voice demanded again from some layer of awareness located in survival reflex, not conscious thought. *Figure it out fast, man, before it's too late!*

Fargo tucked at the knees beside the river growth and moved slowly closer to the men. Again he reminded himself it was none of his picnic, that he might be edging closer to something immensely dangerous, but intense curiosity had him in its grip.

Fargo realized the shoveling had stopped and suddenly the torches were snuffed. Moments later he heard the rata-plan of iron-shod hooves as the men escaped to the north.

But escaping from whom?

Not who, Fargo, urged that body voice deeper than thought. *Escaping from what? Snap into it, Trailsman! Don't you understand what's wrong?*

Fargo halted as his mind, honed by years of deadly scrapes and narrow escapes, frantically assembled the baffling clues. The shovels, the sudden escape, the half-formed words he might or might not have heard correctly: "Shore it up . . . use plenty . . . not too deep . . . more past the bend . . ."

And this sudden, throbbing silence . . .

Silence!

"God*damn*," Fargo abruptly whispered as the important clue he had missed now slammed into him like a fist, something taught to him years ago by an old mountain man: "Watch out, boy, when the insects fall silent."

Fargo realized what was coming and turned on his heel, bolting back toward the juniper thicket as his stomach turned into a ball of ice. Even as he was about to dive into the thicket the peaceful night was split by blinding light and a cracking boom like the promised doom clap of final reckoning.

The earth split open and heaved flames and dirt in a towering column into the sky. Fargo heard the terrified neighing of the Ovaro and felt a searing ripple of heat as the fire surge washed over him before lifting him into the night and flinging him like a child's toy.

You were too late, Fargo, was his last thought before his world closed down to pain and darkness and oblivion. *You were just a few seconds too late!*

2

At some point Fargo realized he wasn't dead. A dead man couldn't feel this much pain.

"Sun's up, Fargo. Rise and shine."

Something kicked the sole of Fargo's boot. With a great effort of will he pried his eyelids open. He saw a blurred vision of bottomless blue sky and smelled the aroma of fried bacon and fresh-brewed coffee.

"You look like death warmed over," said a man's voice beyond his field of vision.

Fargo felt stinging pain all over his body. Groaning at the effort, he rose up on one elbow. The man who had just spoken to him sat on a log nearby, sopping bacon grease off a tin plate with a hunk of saleratus bread.

"I made extra for you," explained the stranger in good English with a Mexican accent. "Hope you don't mind that I helped myself to your eats."

The day went even blurrier as Fargo forced himself to sit up. His white hat lay beside him, and Fargo noticed that it was singed. So were some of the fringes on his buckskin clothing. He also noticed that he was back in his original camp just behind the juniper thicket.

He glanced to his left and saw the Ovaro contentedly munching from a nose bag. Its mane and tail were slightly singed but otherwise the stallion appeared to be in fine fettle.

"I played hell trying to calm him down after the explosion," the stranger said. "That's a magnificent stallion, Fargo. I was tempted to steal him."

Fargo's vision cleared and he peered closer at the man. He was somewhere in his twenties, a mestizo of indeterminate mixed blood, copper-skinned, of medium height and build, with quick-darting, mistrustful eyes set deep behind prominent cheekbones. A black sombrero left half of his smooth-shaven face in shadow.

"So why didn't you steal him?" Fargo retorted.

"That's the kind of horse people notice. And I prefer not to be noticed."

"How do you know my name?"

"I found an old army contract in one of your saddle pockets—something about scouting for a mapping party. I recognized your name right off. You've got a reputation in these parts. My name is Santiago Valdez, by the way."

Santiago Valdez . . . Fargo had heard of him, too, but kept that to himself. He was a noted pistolero and said to possess excellent trailcraft. The son of a Kiowa mother and a Mexican father, there was talk that he was occasionally a hired gun and that he had escaped from jail several times in Mexico.

Fargo took in the man's gun belt trimmed with silver conchos. Two squat, odd-looking revolvers of a type Fargo had never seen rested in cutaway holsters. Both holsters were tied down low on Valdez's thighs.

"A professional, I see," Fargo remarked as he rose unsteadily to his feet.

Valdez set the plate aside and wiped his mouth with the back of his hand.

"If, by 'professional' you mean that I kill for money, then you've got it wrong. But if you mean that I am very good at killing—yes, I'm a professional. Coffee?"

Fargo nodded even though his belly was stirring with nausea. Gingerly he felt his face. He winced when his fingers probed spots that had been burned.

"You'll have to trim your beard," Valdez explained as he handed Fargo a tin cup. "Your eyebrows are singed, too. But your skin burns are minor—nothing a little bear grease won't soothe. You're very lucky—I watched that blast lift you twenty feet into the air."

"You *watched*?" Fargo repeated.

Valdez's strong, perfect teeth flashed when he grinned. "I watched. You might say you were blown 'Skye' high. I dragged you back behind the thicket."

Fargo grunted to acknowledge the pun. "So you were the one I heard riding near here last night. Who are those jaspers who set off that explosion and what the hell for?"

"Never mind who they are. As to the 'what for'—you'll see soon enough although you might not believe your eyes."

Fargo's legs felt rubbery and he sat down, resting his back against his saddle and taking a hissing sip of coffee.

"Obviously you're watching these men," Fargo said. "Are they gringos?"

Valdez nodded.

"What's your dicker with them?" Fargo added. "You a bounty hunter?"

"You ask too many questions."

The Trailsman had seen Valdez's face harden at his query. He realized the man was nursing one hell of a grudge—a killing grudge that was bone deep and personal. This was way beyond money.

"Wha'd'ya mean I might not believe my eyes?" Fargo pressed.

Valdez grinned again. "Quiet down and listen. You notice anything missing?"

For a full minute Fargo did listen. He heard jays scolding, vagrant breezes stirring the nearby cottonwood leaves, the chattering of squirrels. And, yes, something was definitely missing.

"The river current," he finally said, his tone puzzled. "The Rio is close enough to spit in from here, but I can't hear it. That explosion . . . did they dam up the river?"

Again the strong teeth flashed. "Can you walk yet?"

"I'll make myself," Fargo assured him grimly. He set his cup aside and pushed to his feet.

The two men worked their way through the tangle of growth and emerged from the thicket. Fargo's jaw slacked open and he stared upriver—or what *should* have been upriver. There was no dam.

But there was also no Rio Grande. It had simply disappeared.

Fargo stood rooted in numb shock until Valdez's voice jogged him back to awareness.

"It's not really gone, Fargo. That explosion last night, and some careful digging before it, changed the river's course."

Fargo knew the Rio Grande was notorious for jumping its channel. For most of its course—except around the rugged Big Bend region of south-central Texas—it was shallow and slow moving. Natural cycles of drought and flooding had created new channels it sometimes shifted into. But this time it was artificial and purposeful.

Fargo stared across the former riverbed, a slough of mud with countless little pools of water pockmarking it, at a low, rocky ridge.

"After the Mexican War the international boundary," he said, thinking out loud, "was officially established as the exact center of the Rio. That means the long ridge in front of us is now on the American side. And this area is known for having rich veins of silver ore buried under ridges like that."

Valdez nodded. "*Tienes razón*. I see that you know plenty about *la frontera*," he said, using the Spanish name for the border region. "You'll now find that Río Bravo takes a sharp bend around that ridge in an old channel. It flows back into its natural course about two miles downriver from where we're standing."

Fargo swiveled his head to stare at Valdez. "And I see that you know plenty more than I do about what's going on. What is this deal to you?"

"Nothing. They can steal half of Mexico for all I care."

"Nothing, huh? So watching these men so close is just a hobby?"

"As I said, you ask too many questions."

"Yeah," Fargo replied, "and I get too damn few answers."

Valdez's lips firmed. "Then perhaps you should stop asking the questions."

"Would you call that advice or a warning?"

"Is there a difference?" Valdez demanded.

"Plenty. Advice doesn't bother me, and I usually just ignore it. But I don't cotton to warnings—not the kind that shade over into threats."

Valdez stared into those remarkably blue, implacable eyes. Even with his singed beard and eyebrows, his face blistering

7

with burns, Skye Fargo was clearly a man with no more fear in him than a rifle. Santiago Valdez was not easily intimidated, and he wasn't intimidated now. But he respected strength because he believed that strength was the first virtue from which all other virtues sprang.

"I consider it advice," he finally replied. "Which means you will ignore it."

Fargo grinned. "Prob'ly. But right now I'm going to tack my horse and take a closer squint at the blast site."

"Why?" Valdez challenged.

"Now *you're* asking too many questions," Fargo said as the two men headed back to Fargo's camp.

"But what does it matter to you?" Valdez persisted. "You are not the law."

"Neither are you, but you're obviously dogging these men. Let's just say I'm the curious type—especially when I'm blown halfway to the moon."

"Curiosity? That is not a wise thing in *la frontera*."

"Now there we agree," Fargo conceded. "But wisdom isn't my strong suit."

La frontera, Fargo knew from long experience, was far more than simply a border demarcation. It was actually a unique "third country," neither quite Mexican nor quite American. It extended for approximately twenty miles on either side of the long border and featured its own foods, customs and harsh, unwritten laws—even its own hybrid language known as Spanglish. But most of all, as Valdez had just hinted, it was fraught with its own unique dangers.

Valdez drank a second cup of coffee while Fargo packed up his gear and tacked the Ovaro. The mestizo knocked the rawhide hobbles off his sturdy roan gelding and lithely forked leather. Fargo, however, was a bit slower swinging up onto the hurricane deck.

"If I were you, gringo," Valdez said, "I would rest here for a few hours. And that is friendly advice," he hastened to add.

Fargo grinned weakly. "I've been in worse shape. Where you headed?"

"Wherever it is best for me to be," Valdez replied from a deadpan.

Fargo shook his head in wonder as both men cleared the

thicket. "You are the world-beatingest man, Valdez. But I thank you for dragging me back into cover. And good hunting."

Valdez opened his mouth to reply. But all that came out was a harsh grunt of pain when a fire-hardened arrow punched into his left thigh with a sickening sound like a cleaver slicing into a side of raw beef.

3

Santiago Valdez, face twisted with pain, reflexively reached for the arrow, fletched with black crow feathers, protruding from his thigh.

"It's a long way from your heart!" Fargo snapped, reining the Ovaro around in a circle to spot their attackers. "Let it go for now."

Fargo saw the attackers making a beeline toward them from the east in a boiling cloud of yellow-brown dust. He had expected to see an Indian war party, but was forced to do a double take: There were only three men, all apparently white judging from the pale reflections of their faces.

Only three . . . at first Fargo was tempted to handle them with his Henry and its sixteen-round magazine. But just then a bullet snapped past his face, and he realized these were far from average marksmen—still at least four hundred yards out they were nonetheless shooting with near pinpoint accuracy from horseback.

Another arrow whiffed in, this one so close the feather burned Fargo's left temple.

"Make tracks!" Fargo urged the pain-distracted Valdez, slapping the roan hard on its rump. "These ain't no thirty-five-cent bandits!"

Both horses bolted to the west. The unknown archer, Fargo quickly grasped, was the most dangerous of the trio. Despite bouncing atop a galloping horse, he was nocking and firing arrows with a speed and accuracy Fargo had seen only in Comanches.

The Ovaro, well rested and eager to stretch out the night kinks, quickly raced from a gallop to a headlong run, and

Valdez's strong roan did not fall far behind. Fargo had noticed a percussion rifle in the mestizo's saddle sheath, but it was all the wounded man could do to stay in the saddle.

An arrow punched into Fargo's nearside saddlebag, missing his leg by a hairbreadth. Fargo took the reins in his teeth. Plucking his Henry from its boot, he levered a round into the chamber and twisted halfway around to the right. Lodging the rifle's butt plate in his hip socket, he began levering and firing.

Again, again, yet again he levered and fired, watching his bullets kick up dust and adjusting his aim to walk the rounds in closer. Finally, with his seventh or eighth shot, the lead rider's hat went spinning off his head, and the wary trio opted for discretion over valor, reversing their dust. Fargo served them up a few more chaser shots in case they changed their minds.

He reined back slightly, slowing the Ovaro to a canter and allowing an ashen-faced Valdez, who seemed oblivious to everything except pain, to catch up.

"Get your feet back into the stirrups!" Fargo shouted to him. "And hold on! Soon as I find a good spot, we'll rein in and get that arrow point out."

Fargo studied the desolate terrain. This stretch of the borderland was mostly barren and desiccated, the vast, yellow-brown monotony broken only by wiry tufts of palomilla grass, low clumps of prickly pear and the occasional tall, thin cactus known as Spanish bayonets. But it was also crisscrossed by arroyos, and he spotted the mouth of one straight ahead.

Both riders descended into the deep, flash-flood erosion ditch and dismounted, Fargo helping Valdez from the saddle.

"Fargo," the copper-skinned pistolero hissed through gritted teeth, "I've had arrows in me before, and they never hurt like this. *Maldita!* Perhaps it is poison tipped."

"Stretch out on your back," Fargo ordered. He had already glanced at the arrow penetrating his saddlebag. "It's not poison tipped—the point is fashioned from sheet metal. We're going to play hell getting it out—I don't dare shove it through. Least you're not losing much blood. Got any whiskey?"

Valdez was trembling in the early stages of shock. "Off-side saddle pocket," he muttered.

Fargo was surprised when he dug out a bottle of Very Old Pale, distilled especially for American army officers. He made Valdez take the bottle down by a few inches, then snapped the arrow off short and cut a swathe of the cotton trousers away to expose the ugly red pucker of the wound.

"Sheet metal points," he explained as he pulled his Arkansas toothpick from its boot sheath, "tend to clinch tight around bone. You can't just cut them out. Here, knock back some more of this oil of gladness—you're going to need it. I'm going to have to do some cutting to get a better look-see."

Fargo lit several lucifer matches in a row to sterilize the tip of his knife. Knowing that being too careful would only prolong Valdez's agony, he quickly cut out a gobbet of bloody meat for a better view of the interior of the wound.

"Cristo!" Valdez cried out, reverting to Spanish in his agony. *"Quieres matarme?"*

"No, I'm not trying to kill you," Fargo insisted, studying the bloody maw of wound intently. "There, I see how it is. It hit bone, all right, but you got lucky. Most of the arrow's force was spent by the time it reached you, and the point has clinched on only one side. Hold on. . . ."

"Sagrada Virgin!" Valdez moaned, pain screwing his voice up a few octaves. *"Que pena tan fuerte! Ay, Dios!"*

"Stop kicking around," Fargo snapped as he turned to rifle in a saddlebag. "You're making it bleed more, chucklehead."

Fargo pulled out a bundle wrapped in cloth and secured with a rawhide whang. He opened it and selected a fishhook, tying it to a length of catgut thread.

Fargo knelt beside the wounded man again. "Damn it, man, lie still or I can't finish the job."

When Valdez failed to comply, Fargo threw a short, hard jab to the "sweet spot" of the mestizo's jaw, halfway between the earlobe and the point of the chin. Valdez slumped, knocked out cold, and Fargo worked quickly.

After several attempts he managed to hook the clinched side of the arrow point and wiggle it loose before lifting it out. Fargo flushed the wound well with Very Old Pale and packed it tight with flour to clot the blood. Then he swathed it with linen strips and tied them off.

Valdez drifted back to awareness a few minutes later, groaning. But the alcohol was kicking in now, and he no longer floundered like a fish in the bottom of a boat.

Fargo tucked the mangled arrow point into Valdez's shirt pocket. "Keep that for a souvenir. If the wound doesn't mortify in the next day or so, you'll survive. It's going to start bleeding again, though, so you'll need to pack it with flour or gunpowder—beef tallow is even better if you can lay hands on some."

"It feels like you took off my leg."

Fargo lifted Valdez's head so he could knock back another slug of liquor. "Who are those hombres?"

Valdez ignored the question.

"Are they the same ones," Fargo pressed on, "who blasted the river out of its bed last night?"

Valdez still ignored him.

"You ungrateful son of a bitch," Fargo said. "Maybe I *will* lop off that leg."

"Look, I'm grateful, Fargo. I'll tell you this much: You *don't* want to brace any of those three. As you just found out, they are dangerous men. Each was hired for his—how do you say it?—extraordinary skill at killing. Now that they've seen you with me, they will move heaven and earth to kill you. Do the smart thing and put *la frontera* far behind you."

Fargo cursed. "This trail is taking more turns than a cross-eyed cow. Well, since they were nearby I'm going to assume they were in on that blast last night. You say they were hired—are you after them or whoever hired them?"

"Who first made days and gave them to men?"

Fargo tugged at his singed beard. "This is personal with you, right? You're not after those three—you're after whoever has them on his payroll."

"I'm drunk, but not *that* drunk. You're wasting your time trying to prod me. I'll say it again: Your only chance is to clear these parts."

"I'm the one who decides what my chances are. That blast

last night wasn't meant to kill me. But this just now was. And nobody tries to kill me without answering for it. I'm sensitive on that score."

"Fargo, I know about your reputation, and I know you're death to the devil. But you have no idea what you'll find if you're stubborn enough to turn *this* rock over. That's all I have to say, so don't ask me any more questions."

"All right," Fargo surrendered. "I'll button it. I'm more likely to get blood from a turnip than to pry information out of you. But there's something you *can* tell me. . . ."

Fargo slid one of the squat, odd-looking revolvers from Valdez's holster. "I've never seen a gun like this—the hell is it? A foreign model?"

"Yes and no. It was designed by Adams of London, but it's been made in America since 1855 in very limited numbers. It's called double action, but it's still considered experimental. You won't likely see another one."

"Double action?" Fargo replied skeptically. "I've heard talk of such a gun. The army rejected the model they tested because it jams too easy. They concluded it would be ten years, at least, before a reliable one came on the market."

Valdez nodded. "This one jams, too—too many small, moving parts. They have to be cleaned and oiled constantly and the sear bends too easy. You almost have to be a gunsmith to keep it working. It'll be a long time before it replaces that single-action Colt of yours."

"Then if it's half-assed why do you carry it?"

"Because the time required to thumb-cock a revolver can be an eternity in a gunfight, especially when you're facing more than one man."

"There's that," Fargo allowed.

"This Adams double action shoots as fast as I can pull the trigger."

"Sure, if it doesn't jam. Every man to his own gait. Me, I'd rather have a slower barking iron that's dependable than a faster one that's not."

"Why do you think I carry two? I always draw them as a pair. It's not likely they'll both jam at the same exact time."

Fargo holstered the gun again. "Well, whatever you're up to, you're mighty damn serious about it."

"Serious as cancer," Valdez agreed.

Fargo stood up again and tied hobbles on the roan. "You should be safe here. You got food and water?"

"Plenty of water and buffalo jerky."

"All right. I recommend you rest here until at least nightfall. I'm heading out."

"Headed north—way north?" Valdez said hopefully.

"Nope. I'm going to take a close look at that blast site so I can eventually report it to the army up at Fort Union. And then I'm going to pick up the trail of those three skunk-bit coyotes."

"Report it? What's it to you?"

"What, do you need an elephant to sit on you? A chunk of Mexico has just been stolen by gringos—a *rich* chunk of Mexico. This region is already a simmering pot, and it's going to boil over when this gets back to the Mexican government. 'Case you haven't noticed, the border region has been peopling up lately. Do you want the 'forty-seven war to flare up all over again?"

"I tried to help you out," Valdez said. "Now it's your funeral."

"Distinct possibility." Fargo turned a stirrup and forked leather. "But like I said, I don't let any son of a bitch try to kill me and then just ride away like it's none of my business."

"I've heard that about you."

"You heard right," Fargo replied, gigging the Ovaro toward the mouth of the arroyo.

El Paso was a rough frontier town hardly known for its luxurious accommodations. However, it was also a mining center visited by a limited number of ultra-wealthy capitalists. Thus, the one notable exception to its drab boardinghouses and fleapit hotels was the Del Norte Arms on Paseo Street.

This impressive, five-story edifice was constructed of solid fieldstone and featured a parquet-floored lobby, wrought-iron balconies, plaster ornaments on the ceilings and deferential employees in gold-braided livery.

One week before the massive blast that altered the course of the Rio Grande, Santa Fe mining kingpin Stanley Winslowe had reserved the huge suite of rooms that comprised much of the fifth floor. An adjoining room was now occupied by "businessman's agent" Harlan Perry. Late in the afternoon on the day that Mexico had suddenly shrunk by thousands of acres, Perry was visited by three men he proudly referred to as his "intervention team."

"Congratulations are in order, gentlemen," he announced as he handed around imported cigars banded with gilt paper rings and poured out four glasses of bourbon from a crystal decanter. "It's true that we have a couple of flies in the ointment. But you did an exceptional job last night—perfectly executed. Mr. Winslowe has authorized me to pay all of you a generous bonus."

Perry was almost professorial-looking with his gold-rimmed spectacles, neat spade beard and slight, chicken-wing shoulders. Most men with callused hands dismissed him at first glance as a lavender-scented poncy, an impression he carefully cultivated to disguise the ruthless cunning of a man adept at "clearing the profit path" at any cost to innocent human life. His room reeked of eucalyptus fumigation, which he endured three times a week to treat his chronic congestion.

"Yeah, boss, Slim done a good job with that shaped charge," agreed Deuce Ulrick. "But it looks to me like that half-breed Valdez might have help. I'm pretty sure that was Skye Fargo who sided him this morning. Dame Rumor has it that Fargo rode into El Paso yesterday with a caravan."

"It was Fargo," Perry said with certainty as he passed the drinks around. "He was indeed in town, and the description you gave me fits perfectly."

"Fargo is a good man to let alone," fretted Slim Robek. "I was up north when that son of a bitch tracked down and killed the Butcher Boys gang."

Perry nodded. "He and Valdez are both formidable men and we won't take either one of them lightly. However, both men are known to be one-man outfits, and it's too early to conclude that they've teamed up. Valdez, of course, is a permanent impediment that will have to be removed. But Fargo is a drifter, and the popular impression that he is a crusader is hogwash. I suspect he'll move on."

"Maybe so," Ulrick said. "But he might be a witness to what we done. And him being a newspaper hero and all, if he does decide to report what he seen, people will tend to believe him."

"I've considered that. But you say it was dark and he couldn't have seen your faces?"

"Ain't likely."

Perry shrugged. "No rose without a thorn, right? Assuming he even saw you last night, it's good that he can't identify anyone. Eventually someone around here may prove what happened, but Mr. Winslowe has taken steps on that score— the Chinese call it 'gate money.' At any rate, I have the utmost confidence in the three of you, and so does Mr. Winslowe."

Perry's confidence in his carefully assembled team was amply justified by their past performance. He surveyed all of them now as they imbibed, congratulating himself yet again for his resourcefulness.

Deuce Ulrick, Perry's chief lieutenant, was sprawled negligently in a chintz-covered armchair, a draw-shoot artist who had learned to enjoy killing in the charnel house of the Mexican War. He was a strong, barrel-chested man with blue-black beard stubble, dead, flint-chip eyes and a mean slash of mouth like a scar. His brutal appearance belied a good brain, and his take-charge manner made him a natural leader among criminal elements.

Appalachian Slim Robek, six foot four and whipcord thin, stood in the embrasure of a window watching the street below. He was both a dead shot with his Model 1855 Colt revolving cylinder rifle and a superlative explosives expert. His grating, girlish voice and panther-scarred face were off-putting, but the successful explosion last night attested to Perry's canny insights into the worth of men.

Perry's gaze cut to the fourth man in the room, Johnny Jackson. His flat, chinless, deadpan face was unremarkable, but he was unsurpassed in the silent ambush. The expert archer could nock and shoot ten arrows with lethal accuracy while a rifleman was chambering a single round into a breechloader. His Osage-orange–wood bow strung with tough buffalo sinew was copied from the Kiowas, known for the strongest bows on the frontier. His fox-skin quiver was stuffed with fire-hardened arrows tipped with sheet-metal points, each arrow expertly crafted by Jackson himself.

"I have the *utmost* confidence in you three," Perry reiterated, collecting their glasses and filling them again. "The blast last night was crucial to Mr. Winslowe's plans for expansion of his operation. But, as you know, he has also purchased mining rights to a second land parcel that abuts the Rio Grande."

"At Tierra Seca, right?" Deuce Ulrick said.

Winslowe nodded. "And a second blast must come soon. It's best to do these, ahh, reconfigurations of the river in one fell swoop. Fortune favors the bold, not the procrastinators."

"When, boss?"

"I'll be discussing that with Mr. Winslowe. In the meantime you three must concentrate on Valdez."

"Now, see, that's what I don't get," Ulrick said. "You say he's out to kill you. But what the hell for?"

Perry's lips tightened for a moment before he waved this aside. "Let's just say he's on a vengeance quest. You know how these men with Latin blood are—they live for the blood feud."

"He's got Kiowa blood, too," Johnny Jackson pointed out. "Them sons-a-bitches know how to kill a man fifty ways before breakfast."

Perry's bland face turned grim. "Indeed. Which makes it all the more imperative that you kill him as soon as possible. I don't think he's figured out yet where I am—that's why he's watching you three like a cat on a rat."

"I mighta killed him already," Jackson boasted. "I was too far back to see if I hit him in his lights, but he was doubled up in the saddle, all right."

Slim Robek turned away from the window to address the others in his hillman's twang.

"I been studying on this," the Appalachian said in his feminine voice. "A body oughter fret this 'breed sure enough. He's left plenty of widows and orphans. But I'm more afeared of Fargo and what he's fixin' to do. The boss here says Fargo's got no call to stick around these parts and nose in, and could be that's true. But we come nigh to killin' him today, and from what I've heered of Fargo, that's all the call he needs."

"A good point," Perry said. "I said I *suspect* he'll move on, but until we know more I think it might be wise to consider both men equally dangerous. If Fargo does decide to stir things up, he's the type who will want information first. That means he'll have to return to the location of the blast."

"We'll toss out the net," Ulrick said. "If he hangs around here long enough, we'll send him over the mountains, all right."

"No better men for the job," Perry said. "But your remark about his being a newspaper hero, Deuce, has set me thinking. We don't just need to eliminate him—we need to do it quickly before he possibly gets the word out to the wrong authorities. Meaning that perhaps I had better take out some insurance."

"How so?"

"This very day I'm going to send a messenger rider up to Taos."

Ulrick's face suddenly paled and he sat up straighter. "You mean Mankiller?"

"Yes, Mankiller. In fact, his handler is already down here in a strategic location. I made sure of that when Mr. Winslowe explained the importance of this assignment."

"But you know how Mankiller can be, boss."

"I do indeed, Deuce. That's why I'm sending for him."

4

Skye Fargo had carefully pondered the bizarre situation with the deliberate rerouting of the Rio Grande, studying all of its vexing facets.

He could simply follow Santiago Valdez's advice and put *la frontera* far behind him. After all, a myriad of powerful robber barons were already raping the frontier to amass personal fortunes in gold, silver, timber and land, and Fargo knew that no one was going to stop their greedy onslaught— not when the barons had the politicians in their hip pockets.

But this crime had been personalized when those three thugs—obviously on someone's payroll—had tried to snuff his wick. And although Fargo was not possessed of do-gooder instincts, neither could he just ignore the importance of the astounding land grab he had witnessed. One man stealing land from another man was a private feud. But one man stealing land from an entire country, and altering an international border to do so was dangerously provocative in a region that was already a tinderbox of tension, ill will and resentment.

Reluctantly, Fargo concluded that he would have to make a report to Colonel Josiah Evans, commander of Fort Union in the Department of New Mexico. Evans had hired Fargo, earlier that year, as a contract scout for a mapping expedition into the Sangre de Cristo range of the Rockies.

The two men had not exactly hit it off, Evans being a rule-book commander who considered Fargo too undisciplined and disrespectful of authority. But Fargo considered Evans honest and upright and perhaps likely to follow through forcefully when he learned what had happened.

That meant Fargo had to act on his resolve to study that blast site up close. But after the attack on him and Santiago

Valdez, he decided to wait a day. He spent that night in a cold camp on the Mexican side of the border just north of the sleepy pueblo of El Porvenir.

He rolled out of his blanket just before sunrise and ate a spartan meal of hardtack soaked in coffee. He had grained and watered the Ovaro the night before, and Fargo rode out as the bloodred sun was breaking over the eastern flats.

The country surrounding him was hot, dry and dusty, dotted with ocotillo and greasewood and the occasional oddly twisted Joshua tree. But magnificent purple mountain ranges were visible on the far horizons. Fargo favored desolate, open terrain like this—visibility was excellent and a man who remained vigilant could see anyone approaching well beyond rifle range.

And Fargo did remain vigilant. Ruthless Mexican bandit gangs crisscrossed the borderland, and they would murder a man for his boots much less a fine stallion like the Ovaro. More importantly, Fargo had a healthy respect for the trio that attacked him and Valdez yesterday. A moment's carelessness around them, and Fargo knew his bones would end up bleaching with so many others in the desert sand.

About a mile south of the Rio Grande's new course, Fargo encountered an old peasant on a burro.

"Que tal, viejo," Fargo greeted him.

The old man, his face sere and wrinkled like a dry chamois from a lifetime in the sun, was polite but wary. *"Buenos dias."*

Fargo was curious to know if the word was spreading about the river. He cobbled an awkward sentence together in his limited Spanish. *"Anteanoche—escuche usted un gran sonido como una bomba?"*

The peasant seemed to understand that Fargo was asking if he had heard the blast night before last. He nodded and replied in halting Spanglish.

"Caramba, senor! *El* Río Bravo, she is now *muy* close *a mi casa! Es* the work of *el* diablo."

The work of *three* devils, Fargo thought. And, likely, even bigger devils behind the scene.

"Tobacco?" the old-timer said hopefully.

Fargo gave him one of his skinny black cigarillos and tipped his hat before moving on.

Fargo aimed for the familiar low ridge that was now located on the American side of the shifted border. He reined in and pulled the 7X army binoculars from his saddlebag, minutely studying the terrain in every direction.

"Looks all right," he finally announced to the Ovaro, who tossed his head and snorted.

Still, something felt wrong to Fargo.

He gigged the Ovaro toward the new bend where the Rio began its long detour around the silver-bearing ridges. First he splashed his stallion through the muddy water to the American side of the former riverbed.

"Christ," Fargo muttered.

It was only the second day since the Rio Grande had been explosively rerouted, yet already the many puddles had evaporated and the mud was baking into cracked clay. Within a week or so it would look like many other old channels of the Rio—disguising the fact that the river had not jumped its channel naturally.

The blast site, however, was still detectable. Fargo swung down and tossed the reins forward. But something still felt off-kilter to him. Out of an abundance of caution he wrapped an arm around the Ovaro's neck and tugged him toward the ground.

Horses rarely lay down except to enjoy a roll or when sick. But the well-trained Ovaro had been taught to go down and stay down until Fargo whistled him up. Fargo had found the trick especially useful when attacked on the open plains. Recalling the superb marksmanship of that trio yesterday morning, he decided to lower the Ovaro's target profile. A man set afoot in this terrain didn't stand a Chinaman's chance against that bunch.

Fargo studied the blast area up close. The old channel into which the river had been sent had been deepened by digging at its beginning to facilitate the jump—he could tell that by the slightly darker color of newly turned earth just above the slow-moving current. That color difference, too, would soon fade.

Also, whoever set the large charge knew exactly what he was doing. The blast had moved a wall of dirt forward to impede the old course. But at a casual glance it simply looked like natural riverbank.

The Rio Grande flowed steadily by with a soft murmur like the soughing of a light breeze in treetops. Nearby a flock of crows had settled down to drink, raising a ruckus of scrawking. They suddenly scattered, and Fargo realized he had been so busy he hadn't looked around for at least five minutes.

He looked back over his shoulder toward the west and cursed his green-antlered stupidity. A few hundred yards out was a low, wind-scrubbed knoll he had studied with his binoculars. Three riders had spurted out from behind it and now bore down on him.

Fargo had faced every manner of danger so often that he could instantly calculate survival odds. He could simply hop his horse and flee, counting on the Ovaro's superior speed and stamina to outrun the danger. But the three outlaws already had up a head of steam, and the odds were too great, given their marksmanship skills, that they could drop his horse.

He could also spread flat in a prone position, lowering his target profile, and rely on the Henry to dissuade them. But while the typical marksman would find a prone man a difficult target, Fargo believed it would be the kiss of death to give these men a stationary target of any kind.

The rifleman opened up first, his weapon making insignificant popping sounds at this distance. But his first slug tugged hard as it passed through the folds of Fargo's shirt, and the Trailsman went into evasive action.

He levered the Henry, held it tight against his chest, and tucked and rolled fast, moving several yards before coming up to an offhand-kneeling position and firing back. He knew his only chance, against shooters this formidable, was to constantly force them to a new bead.

He fired, tucked, levered while rolling, and popped up to fire again. Now bullets and arrows stitched the ground all around him, and Fargo desperately tried to drop a bead on the middle horse. But the heavy, accurate, sustained fire kept him in constant motion and made it supremely risky to stay in a firing position for more than a second.

"Who *are* these bastards?" he muttered when an arrow whiffed past his ear with a sound like a bumblebee.

Fargo realized this was a Mexican standoff he could not win without taking a huge risk. The next time he rose on one knee to fire, he took an extra two seconds to drop his sights in the middle of the horse's chest. A thin curlicue of blood snaked out and the horse crashed to the ground, sending its rider cartwheeling down with it.

But these killers were unflappable. While the skinny rake with the rifle helped the shaken rider onto his own horse, the archer kept Fargo rolling madly for his life. The men reined back around into the desert haze.

Fargo resisted the strong temptation to fire on them while they escaped. Between this attack and the narrow escape yesterday, he had depleted too many of the Henry's shells. He might need every bullet he had if they jumped him again before he could ride into El Paso.

The Trailsman rose unsteadily to his feet and retrieved his hat, using it to whack at the dust coating his buckskins.

"Who *are* they?" he repeated in a tone of wonder.

He tried to whistle the Ovaro up, but fear had dried his mouth.

Fargo rode out to the spot where the downed horse lay. He had hoped it was dead, but its exposed side heaved like a bellows in death agony and a bloody pink froth bubbled from the claybank's nostrils. Shot in a lung, Fargo realized.

He swore without heat. He hated like hell to shoot a horse, but his hand had been forced. And now he had to shoot it again.

His lips a grim, determined slit, Fargo drew his Colt and put a bullet in the dying animal's brain, instantly ending its suffering. The offside saddlebag was trapped under the dead horse, but Fargo opened the nearside pocket hoping for some clue to the rider's identity.

All he found, however, was a shoeing hammer and a spare set of horseshoes. These were professional killers who knew better than to leave helpful clues behind. The saddle was simple and functional in the style of the Mexican vaqueros, with *tapaderos* covering the stirrups to protect the rider's feet in cactus and heavy brush.

By now, the morning was well advanced and the sun radiated furnace heat. Sweat beaded in Fargo's hair but evaporated before it could pour onto his forehead.

The trail of the two escaping riders was clear in the desert hard pack. Fargo followed it due west on the American side for two miles, the Rio in constant sight on his left. He held the Ovaro to a trot, letting that deadly trio get well out ahead of him. Fargo wasn't eager for another cartridge session in open country like this where he was exposed like a bedbug on a clean sheet. Another mile and he was convinced they were headed to a little border hole-in-the-wall known as Tierra Seca.

But would they just pass through or wait there for him?

Fargo knew the place and didn't welcome the prospect. The borderland was rife with outcast settlements populated, at any given time, by *contrabandistas*, owlhoots of various stripes, mystics, prophets, mixed-breeds and enterprising, freelance whores adverse to turning their earnings over to pimps and madams. Fargo had even heard, from an amused merchant on the recent caravan, that there was a newly arrived commune of "agricultural utopians" in Tierra Seca who preached peace, equality and free love.

Recalling the "free love" angle perked Fargo up in the saddle. After all, that was the only kind he subscribed to.

However, his revived mood degenerated into more curses when Fargo encountered a long bull train coming from the direction of Tierra Seca. The little settlement was located on a transport road between El Paso and the supply depot at Van Horn, Texas. The giant wheels of the freight wagons, and the scores of bulls, had obliterated the tracks Fargo was following.

Still, he spotted no tracks veering off to either side, so they were almost certainly headed toward Tierra Seca.

Fargo's pulse quickened as he reckoned the potential danger. Maybe they expected an experienced tracker to tail them, and maybe they were holed up in the settlement right now waiting to perforate his liver. There would be no law to stop them, nor would any witnesses give a tinker's damn—death, in the borderland, was violent, quick and unremarkable, and the only undertakers were the buzzards.

But the gambler in Fargo knew how things were: In order to win big you had to bet big, even if it was your own life you were wagering.

The Rio Grande made a long curve, and at the beginning of that curve, practically falling into the river, Fargo spotted the drab sight of Tierra Seca. There were a handful of puddled-adobe buildings, perhaps an equal number of knocked-together she-bangs and *jacals*, dwellings made of woven brush. Trash lay scattered in the road, including animal entrails attracting swarms of flies. The constant buzzing set Fargo's teeth on edge.

But a new and impressive sight also greeted him: well-irrigated fields of corn and beans and squash being worked by men and women, most of them gringos. Fargo had to suppress a bark of laughter: Every one of them—even the men—were dressed only in loose sheaths of sewn burlap sacks.

"There's the utopians," Fargo remarked to his stallion, who loosed a whinny that sounded, to Fargo, like a derisive laugh.

"Yeah," Fargo agreed. "Men in dresses—it's enough to make a horse blush."

Fargo quickly, however, focused his wary gaze on the buildings and the spaces between and behind them as he rode closer. He decided to dismount and lead the Ovaro in by the bridle reins, ready to leap behind his horse if gunfire erupted—although there'd be no warning at all if that lethal archer opened up on him.

"Hey there! Hey, long-tall!"

The voice was feminine, melodic, friendly. Fargo glanced to his left and spotted a slender girl so shapely that even her burlap sheath couldn't downplay her ample charms. She was hoeing a row of beans but walked toward the road to meet him.

"Well, now," Fargo greeted her, tipping his hat. "I hope you're the welcoming committee. It's hard to believe a gal can wear burlap and look as good as you do."

"Burlap chafes a mite," she replied. "Whenever I can I just go naked."

She gave him an inviting smile and Fargo felt a tickle of loin heat. The girl was around twenty with Prussian blue eyes, thick, luxuriant, burnt-sienna hair and soft, full lips like cherries ready to be plucked.

"My lands!" she exclaimed after peering closer at him. "It appears that you were recently caught in a fire. Your beard and eyebrows are singed—your hat and clothing, too. I hope you weren't badly hurt."

"Got drunk and rolled into my campfire," Fargo lied. "Looks like you folks have some nice fields growing here."

She beamed proudly. "Yes, thanks to the river. We are continuing the Brook Farm tradition."

"Brook Farm?" Fargo repeated politely while keeping his eyes on the surroundings. "I never heard of the Brook family."

"Not the Brook family, silly. It was an agricultural commune named after a nearby brook. It was very famous."

"I never heard of it," Fargo admitted. "I don't get around too many newspapers."

"You've not heard of it? Goodness, you must be a true hermit! It was a wonderful community that started in Massachusetts in 1841. Many famous people joined. Even Nathaniel Hawthorne lived there for a time."

"Him I've heard of," Fargo said. "So these folks were farmers, huh?"

Her voice grew excited and took on the reverent tone of true believers. "Oh, it was much more than just farming. It was a self-sustaining community. Everyone shared equally in the work and in the pay. And all members were equal. All property was shared and violence abolished."

Fargo struggled to keep a straight face. "Seems like you should've gone there instead of this desert that you have to irrigate. Mighty pretty country in Massachusetts. You folks sure don't look like you're from around here."

"I'm from Hannibal, Missouri. My birth name is Carrie Stanton, but my rebirth name is Peace Child. I couldn't live at Brook Farm, goose, because the main buildings burned down and the community disbanded when I was still a little girl. We call our group here the Phalanx and we make up about half the residents of Tierra Seca."

"Peace Child," Fargo repeated. "Now that's a nice name."

He was lying through his teeth and biting his lip to keep from laughing in her face. He had nothing against farming or peace, but *rebirth name*? This gal was a bigger fool than God made her, but He was mighty kind to her otherwise. She had the face of an angel, the body of a courtesan, and the seductive smile and eyes of a wanton.

"You share *everything*?" he hinted.

She caught his drift and her eyes fixated with fascination on the pup tent in his trousers.

"Everything," she assured him, her voice suddenly throaty. "We do not suppress our desires, and we have abolished jealousy and possessiveness. We view our bodies as vessels of pleasure."

"Well, in that case—"

"Peace Child!"

Fargo glanced behind the girl, who whirled around as a man, also dressed in the ridiculous commune garb, approached them.

"A rest break hasn't been called," he told the girl while watching Fargo from suspicious eyes.

"I just stopped to chat for a minute. This gent is—"

She paused, looking a question at Fargo. "Why, I don't know your name."

"Fargo. Skye Fargo."

"Well! Skye is a mighty pretty name. Skye, this is Ripley Parker."

"My rebirth name," he reminded her, "is Justice. Our old names belong to the venal, violent, greedy world we left behind."

The man spoke with a soft Virginia drawl, but Fargo suspected there was nothing soft about him or his commanding manner. His obsidian eyes burned with the intensity of men who brooked no defiance, and those lumps of scar tissue around them betokened the violent world he had just claimed to repudiate. So did his nose, which had obviously been broken at least twice.

"The others are working diligently," he told Carrie. "You should be too."

"I'm just curious," Fargo said in his amiable manner. "Peace Child here just told me no one's in charge in this Phalanx doohickey of yours. Seems to me you're being a mite bossy . . . Justice."

"Justice is our spiritual leader," Carrie Stanton explained. "We don't believe in the Christian God, but we believe there is spirituality in nature. Anyhow, hope I'll see you around, Skye," she added in a tone of unmistakable invitation.

The "spiritual leader" turned and followed her back into the field.

"Interesting," Fargo muttered.

5

Fargo, drawing plenty of curious and hostile stares, moved carefully around the flyblown settlement until he was certain the outlaw trio were nowhere around. Then he made his way toward the largest adobe building. Several horses and two burros were tied off out front including a well-muscled roan gelding he recognized immediately.

He looped the Ovaro's reins around a crooked snorting post out front and stepped through a doorless arch into a bare-bones cantina that smelled like a bear's cave. He spotted Santiago Valdez eating tortillas and beans at a crude plank counter.

"How's the leg?" Fargo greeted him.

"Hurts like hell. I had trouble with it seeping blood until I took your advice and got some beef tallow from Antonio here. I packed the hole good and it's sealed up tight now."

Fargo glanced around the smoky, dark interior. About a dozen men, most of them Mexican and mestizo, were seated at crude deal tables. They sized him up from caged eyes. One met Fargo's gaze and then contemptuously spat on the packed-dirt floor.

"Friendly place," Fargo remarked. His eyes lingered on a dusky, voluptuous Mexican beauty seated at a corner table with an older woman. She gave Fargo a beguiling smile, but her dark, dangerous eyes watched him with something more intense than flirtatiousness.

"Keep your eyes to all sides or they'll shoot you in the back," Valdez said cheerfully, mopping up the last of his chili beans with a flap of tortilla.

The round-faced proprietor, dressed in dirty white linen and a straw Sonora hat, nodded at Fargo from the other side of the counter.

"Fargo, meet Antonio Two Moons. Besides owning this—how you say?—thriving establishment, he makes and peddles whiskey to Indians. He's also a good barber. Maybe he can trim that burned beard of yours."

"*Una copa*, senor?" Two Moons asked Fargo.

Fargo nodded. He knew these dusty borderland watering holes never served beer, always his first choice. But the milky cactus liquor called pulque went down smoothly and gave a man a pleasant jolt.

Fargo also knew the ritual when ordering a first drink, and he drank his wooden cup to the dregs without pause. Now he was free to sip the second cup at his own pace.

Antonio Two Moons watched him expectantly, as did several others. Fargo pressed a fist into his sternum, emitting a loud belch and reducing some of the tension in the room. Not to do so, in a poor establishment like this, was construed as an insult to the host.

"I see you know the customs," Valdez remarked.

"Yeah, but there's still a helluva lot I don't know about. Why don't you enlighten me?"

Valdez's quick-darting eyes shifted away. His lips twitched in what Fargo guessed was a smile. "*Vaya, hombre.* What can I tell the famous Trailsman?"

Fargo kept his voice low. "For starters, you can tell me what the hell's going on around here. A couple days ago an explosion damn near puts me on the moon and changes the international border. Not long after, you and me almost get shot to rag tatters. Today the same demented jackals jump me again. Now that hot little senyoreeter in the corner appears to be spying on me—or maybe us. Top of all that, there's a bunch of moon-crazy, peace-preaching utopian mush brains hereabouts led by a man who looks about as peaceful as a scalp dance."

Valdez nodded. "So, you met Ripley Parker. . . . I see that the two of us size him up about the same." Valdez added a sly grin. "Did you also . . . 'meet' Peace Child?"

Fargo grinned back. "You too, huh? She's a mite strange but seems willing. I take it you know her in the Biblical sense?"

"Haven't had the chance. Parker watches her like a dog with a bone."

"Dogs are easy to kick. Look, I s'pose it's just a coincidence that I tail three killers to this roach pit and find you here, too?"

"*Quien sabe?* You did a good job in that shoot-out this morning. I had you down for a dead man. Looks like those newspaper sissies aren't just chewing their lips when they talk you up big."

Fargo stared at him. "You mean you watched it? Thank you all to hell and back for pitching into the game."

"You didn't need me. Your guts were showing all over the place."

"Yeah, they damn near were," Fargo shot back sarcastically.

"I would've helped if you required it," Valdez assured him. "This one time. I owe you that much for the surgery you did on my leg."

"All right. If you figure you owe me, then tell me who they are and who hired them."

"That ship has sailed, Fargo. You can ask me questions until you're blue in the face. I got nothing to say."

The Mexican girl was still watching Fargo with unrelenting vigilance.

Valdez pushed away from the counter and hitched up his gun belt with its two odd-looking, experimental revolvers Valdez claimed were double action—a claim Fargo had trouble believing. He clapped on his sombrero.

"Actually," he said, "I *will* tell you something that you've already guessed. I don't give a damn about those three men. And you shouldn't either unless you want to get your life over in a hurry."

"For a man who doesn't give a damn about them you sure seem to be glomming them mighty close."

"You've already guessed right about that, too. They're just the bread crumbs that I have to follow. Fargo, you're dancing on a powder keg."

"And you aren't?"

"I have a good reason. A damn good reason—the best in the world. You've just got a long nose. Point your bridle away from the border while you're still above the horizon."

He walked out before Fargo could reply. The moment

31

Valdez stepped outside, the pretty Mexican girl with the trouble-seeking eyes got up to join Fargo.

"*Buenas tardes*, Senor Fargo."

She looked even better close up. But the haughty beauty's pursed lips were twisted in obvious scorn.

"You have the advantage on me, Senorita . . . ?"

"Velasquez. Rosario Velasquez."

"Pleased, I guess. You seem to have a great interest in me"

"*Por qué* no? You are much man."

"Uh-huh. But your interest in me doesn't seem like the type a much man should welcome."

She tossed back her head and laughed—a silvery smooth, rippling laugh that moved up and down the bumps of Fargo's spine on tiny, tickling feet.

"Oh, but I am much woman, too, *verdad*?"

"Very true," Fargo agreed.

"Some say you ride with Santiago Valdez. Is this so?"

"What if it is true?"

"*Entonces, eres un muerto.*"

Fargo's scratch Spanish was good enough to translate that one: "Then you are a dead man." Two warnings, back to back, predicting Fargo's imminent death. He was glad he wasn't a squeamish man.

"You're much woman, all right," Fargo said. "But there are female scorpions, too."

Again that silvery laugh that sent tingles through Fargo's groin. "Good. I see that we understand each other."

Fargo snatched his hat off the plank bar. "Lady," he assured her before he walked out, "there ain't a *damn* thing around here that I understand."

Only a few hours after Fargo was in Tierra Seca being mysteriously warned by Rosario Velasquez, businessman's agent Harlan Perry conferred with his employer in El Paso's Del Norte Arms hotel.

"The initial steps at my end," said mining kingpin Stanley Winslowe, "have gone quite well. The governor of Chihuahua was quite happy with the, ah, inducement I gave him."

"I trust it wasn't a lump sum," Perry said. "I've dealt with Torres before. He's more or less reliable so long as the carrot is kept dangling in front of his nose. But he burned me once when I was ignorant enough to pay him everything in advance."

Winslowe chuckled. He was a portly, balding man with a gold-chain monocle and salt-and-pepper muttonchop whiskers. His elegant tailoring disguised a shabby morality.

"Don't worry, Harlan. I've dealt with these greasers before. I made it clear that the initial payment will be repeated every month so long as my operation is pulling ore out of those ridges."

Perry nodded. "Well played. Given the constant revolutionary fever in Mexico and the extraordinary weakness of their federal government it should be safe enough for you. Chihuahua is essentially Juan Torres's private little fiefdom."

Winslowe poured himself another glass of scotch and rolled a sip around in his mouth. His luxurious hotel suite featured textured walls and heavy teak furnishings.

"Oh, he'll eventually try to put the crusher on me," he said. "And the U.S. government might butt in at some point. But my engineer tells me the veins under those ridges are dense and high yielding. It won't take that long to mine plenty of high-grade ore. Even if they eventually haze me out, I'll have millions in the banks back east."

The smug satisfaction on Winslowe's face gave way to a frown as a possible irritant occurred to him. "But what's this about this drifter Skye Fargo? Do you really believe he could make trouble?"

"Making trouble is his hallmark. At this point, however, I consider him a volatile unknown quantity. He's put himself into the mix, and he'll have to be killed as soon as possible."

"If he's the fiddle-footed drifter you claim he is, perhaps he'll soon just move on. I hear the man is a bunch quitter."

"That's my understanding, too," Perry replied. "But there's a complicating factor, and his moving on may not be enough."

Winslowe waited expectantly for a few moments and then narrowed his eyes. "Well?" he demanded. "Is there a chicken bone caught in your throat?"

"It's this way, Mr. Winslowe. You may have arranged things with Governor Torres, but the U.S. Army is a horse of a different color. And Fargo has valuable acquaintances in the army."

"If it comes to that, I happen to know you've paid off several high-ranking officers in the past."

Perry nodded. "Yes, even many West Point men often prefer the color gold over red, white and blue."

"Then why the long face?"

"The commander at the nearest fort, Colonel Josiah Evans at Fort Union, is one of these straight-and-narrow types who is pathologically law abiding. I know that from rueful personal experience—he had me indicted once for attempted bribery. Fortunately for me, the judge in the case *was* corruptible."

Winslowe, not liking the drift of this conversation, pushed out of his overstuffed easy chair and began pacing the spacious room.

"You've got good men on the payroll," he pointed out. "Look how professionally they handled the blast. Don't you have confidence in them?"

"I'm confident they're very good, yes. But I learned long ago to respect a worthy enemy. Deuce Ulrick and his men have clashed twice with Fargo to no avail. Just today I had to purchase a new horse for Ulrick—Fargo killed his mount this morning."

Winslowe interrupted his pacing to stare at his subordinate. "I don't like what I'm hearing, Harlan. We need to get moving on this second operation at Tierra Seca. If it's done quickly enough, no one can easily prove that the Rio Grande didn't simply jump its channel naturally at two locations more or less simultaneously. It has done that before."

"Yes, but Tierra Seca poses a problem the first blast didn't—the settlement there hugs the river and there will be people killed, many of them Americans."

"People? Stuff! The dregs of humanity, you mean. No one will miss them or give a damn about them. As for any survivors, they will simply move on to some other filthy sewer. But we can't have a loose cannon like Skye Fargo gumming up the works."

Perry hadn't told his boss about a second loose cannon named Santiago Valdez, nor did he plan to. It was Perry's job to eliminate problems, not create them. And he had definitely created a huge one in Valdez.

"Fargo must be eradicated," Perry agreed. "And while I believe our own men can do the job, I also believe that the best way to hit the mark is to aim above it. I've sent word up to Taos."

Winslowe's brow furrowed in puzzlement. "Taos? Why? I don't—"

Winslowe suddenly caught on and an ashen pallor suffused his face. "You don't mean—?"

"No names," Perry hastened to cut him off. "You'll have nothing to do with it."

Winslowe was forced to return to his chair. He sat down heavily and removed a handkerchief from his inside coat pocket, mopping his brow.

"Christ, Harlan. I know we face a problem. But you-know-who is a dog off his leash—a *mad* dog. I assume you recall what he did in central Texas?"

Harlan Perry did indeed recall that incident, and who could ever forget it? A Texas prosecutor and former Texas Ranger with a stubborn streak of honesty in him had threatened to shut down several of Winslowe's mines for graft and other charges. Mankiller had removed that thorn, all right—along with his wife and three children, two of them still infants.

"Harlan," Winslowe added in a voice just above a whisper, "he *ate* their damn hearts!"

Perry nodded, his bespectacled, professorial face grim.

"That's because he has strange ideas derived from some sort of pagan witchcraft," he explained to his employer.

"Who the hell cares why? The cause is secret, but the effect is known. If he goes off the rails again, he could sink us both—sink us six feet closer to hell."

"Without question," Perry conceded. "Remember, he's only our ace in the hole. I spoke at length with his handler—the only man with some influence over him. I emphatically insisted that there cannot be a repeat of that Texas situation. Also remember, Mr. Winslowe, that Deuce and the others are on the job. Only if they fail will I unleash the final option. One thing is certain: The man from Taos has never failed."

"No," Winslowe agreed in a weak voice, mopping his face again. "And neither did Attila the Hun."

6

Skye Fargo spent his third night in the borderland camped in a deep draw a few miles north of Tierra Seca. He needed to ride into El Paso to replenish his ammo and food supplies, but first he wanted to see Carrie Stanton—"reborn" as Peace Child—and satisfy his curiosity on a few points. And given the curvaceous beauty's seductive flirtation with him the day before, he hoped to satisfy another pressing need.

Fargo rolled out at sunrise and watered the Ovaro from a goatskin bag tied to his saddle horn. Then he carefully inspected the stallion's hooves, removing a few thorns and small stones with a hoof-pick. By then it was light enough for a careful inspection of his surroundings through his binoculars.

Wary of that unholy trio, Fargo scanned the arid country in every direction, searching for movement or reflections more than shapes. All he spotted, however, was a lumbering armadillo and a few scavenging coyotes.

Feeling safe for the moment, Fargo gathered up enough dead mesquite wood to build a cooking fire. He made coffee and fried up the last of his bacon to ease the gnawing in his belly. Then he rode out onto the desert hardpan and pointed his bridle toward Tierra Seca. Already the heat was rising and forming blurry, dancing snakes on the distant horizon.

For a few moments Fargo wondered where those three menacing attackers were holing up. Most hired dirt workers were town men by choice, their trailcraft weak. These three, however, seemed adept at using terrain to their advantage, and he feared they would prove more proficient than the usual greasy-sack outfit at movement and concealment.

They were obviously of a higher caliber, and that meant that whoever was the head of this snake was, too. Mining interests were behind that brazen rerouting of the Rio, and that meant deep pockets. But what the hell, Fargo wondered again, was Santiago Valdez's mix in this deal?

As Fargo trotted his stallion closer to Tierra Seca, he idly observed that the Mexican side of the river rose into low ridges exactly like the area near the blast site. But an impressive sight distracted his thoughts: members of the Phalanx already working the fields. Despite their foolish notions and laughable costumes, these agricultural utopians were certainly industrious.

As he had hoped, Carrie spotted him riding in and walked out to meet him.

"Glad you stuck around," she greeted him. "I hope I had something to do with that. You've sure been on my mind."

Fargo swung down from the saddle. "Same here. There's something we need to take care of, don't you think?"

"Why not right now, long-tall?"

Fargo grinned. "You mean right here?"

She slugged him playfully on the arm. "We don't share *that* much around here." She nodded toward a nearby cornfield. "Notice how the corn is tasseled—it's real high now. Would you like me to show you that field?"

"There's a little farmer in all of us," Fargo assured her. "But I need to get my horse away from the road."

They headed down a row of the bean field, Fargo leading the Ovaro, who kept trying to chomp at the plants.

"Just curious," Fargo said. "Won't Rip—uh, I mean Justice— interfere again when he sees you're not working?"

"Oh, he's still in bed. He sleeps late."

"I thought you all shared equally in the work."

"Well, see, Ripley doesn't really work. He sorta . . . guides the rest of us."

Fargo thought he detected resentment in her tone. "In other words he's privileged? A little more equal than everyone else?"

She shrugged her slim shoulders. "He does seem a little bossy. Danny Dexter wasn't like that. He was our last spiritual leader. His rebirth name was Harmony and he always worked alongside the rest of us. But one day he just up and disappeared without so much as a fare-thee-well. We were fortunate that Justice came along."

"Disappeared, you say? How long after that did Ripley Parker join the group?"

She cast those wing-shaped, Prussian blue eyes at Fargo, searching his face. "Why, a day or so later, I suppose. Why do you ask?"

"No reason," Fargo lied. "I guess it's just a coincidence. How long ago was that when Parker arrived here?"

"Justice," she corrected him. "Only about a week ago. But we all saw right away that he's a highly spiritual man."

Spiritual . . . was that the scar tissue around his eyes, Fargo wondered, or the twice-broken nose?

They approached a wispy, green-eyed blonde who was busy pulling weeds.

"Hi, Peace Child," she said, ogling the tall, buckskin-clad stranger. "Who's your new friend?"

"Skye Fargo, this is Abigail Bartlett. Her rebirth name is Hope."

"You two headed for the cornfield?" Abigail teased. "Remember, Peace Child—it's share and share alike."

"I'm not hogging him. But I met him first. You'll have to wait your turn."

"Well, can I come along and just watch you two?"

Fargo's face brightened. "Say, that sounds—"

"No, you can't," Carrie told her friend. "I'm too bashful for that."

"Well, now," Fargo said, suddenly feeling like a dog in a butcher shop, "this is definitely a fertile field."

They reached the edge of the corn. Fargo led the Ovaro a few yards into the field and tied hobbles on him. The stallion, who had once gnawed tar paper off a shack during starving times in a winter storm up on the northern plains, began contentedly cropping at a corn stalk.

Carrie tugged Fargo a little deeper into the field. Her voice grew husky with the force of suddenly released lust.

"I've been wanting to feel your pizzle inside me ever since I saw how hard it got yesterday," she told him, stroking the swollen furrow bulging his trousers. "Mercy! It's so big and I can feel it throbbing so hard! I'm gonna work it nice, Skye."

She lifted her arms to pull the burlap sheath off, and with

one quick whisk she stood completely naked before him. Fargo drank in the erotic sight: the luxuriant waves of reddish-brown hair; the pouting, ripe cherry lips; the firm tits with pink, slightly upturned nipples; the alabaster skin like a creamy lotion, gently rounded stomach, and flaring hips with a silken "V" of mons hair centered between them.

Even more hot blood surged into Fargo's iron-hard man-hood as Carrie spread her sheath on the ground and lay on her back, spreading the ivory thighs wide apart to goad him on with the sight of her most intimate parts. One eager hand began to cosset her chamois-enfolded pearl, swelling it out into clear view.

"Hurry, Skye!" she begged him. "Put it in me and stroke me fast and hard! Oh, I'm gonna work it *so* nice for you!"

Fargo, hotter than a branding iron himself, dropped his gun belt, then his trousers, and fitted himself into his favorite saddle, letting her grab his man-gland and guide it inside of her hot, slippery, tight sex. They both gasped at the galvanic charge of pleasure when Fargo flexed his buttocks hard and drove into the deepest center of her womanhood.

She hadn't lied to Fargo when she promised him she'd work it nice for him. Her love muscle was strong and greedy, and she rapidly squeezed and released, squeezed and released, charging Fargo up to a furious frenzy as he pounded the saddle ever faster and harder. Carrie, charged right up with him, began writhing like a whirling dervish as a nearly unbroken string of climaxes washed over her in tidal waves.

Fargo went into the strong finish, cupping his hands under her firm, satin-smooth ass and lifting her off the ground as he made his conclusive thrusts, explosively spending himself.

Their mutual release left both of them limp rag dolls for several minutes.

"My stars and garters," she finally managed to gasp. "You must have taken lessons."

"You've been to school yourself," Fargo replied, sitting up and closing his fly.

"Skye?"

"Hmm?"

"How come you asked me about Rip—I mean, Justice?"

"Because I don't much like him," Fargo said frankly. "I got the impression he's sailing under false colors."

"What do you mean?" she pressed him.

"Like I said—it's just an impression."

She averted her eyes. "He bothers me, too. He's pushing the rest of us around too much, but everybody's afraid to speak up."

"I'm gonna be watching him," Fargo assured her. "Now can I ask you a question? What do you know about Rosario Velasquez?"

Carrie stood up in a huff and wiggled into her sheath.

"Oh, I see how it is. You waited until *after* you screwed me to ask about her. Were you thinking about her while we did it?"

Fargo struggled to keep a straight face. "Hold on here, cupcake. Whatever happened to all this share and share alike and 'we abolished jealousy' business?"

"Oh, pouf! All that's fine when I know I'm the prettiest girl. Rosario is a real beauty. All the men want her."

"I'm not looking to poke her," Fargo lied, adding truthfully, "but she's up to something. There's something dangerous about that woman."

"I don't know how dangerous she is, but I know she likes bad men—brutal, violent men. There's one who comes to see her now and then. . . . I was working in the field a few days ago when he dragged a Mexican out of the cantina and beat him up so bad it was hours before the poor man could even stand up."

"This brutal man—is he a Mexican himself?"

She shook her head. "He's an American. I only saw him at a distance that one time."

"Does he ride into Tierra Seca with two companions?"

Again she shook her head. "I don't know. But Rosario watched the beating and egged him on. Then she took him back to her house, and they were laughing about it."

"Interesting," Fargo said.

"Skye, *why* are you asking all these questions? Are you a lawman?"

"Not hardly. I'm just the curious sort. Tell me, Car— Peace Child. Have you folks here at the farm heard anything about the Rio Grande lately?"

"No. Should we have?"

Fargo ignored the question. He was afraid to tell her about that explosion rechanneling the river for fear she'd say something to the wrong person. And right now it was impossible to know who the wrong person might be.

He buckled on his gun belt while she watched him thoughtfully. Her eyes slid down to look at the Arkansas toothpick in his boot. "That's a scary-looking knife."

"It's common on the frontier. Mighty handy. It'll soften up bed ground, serve as a hammer and cut branches for firewood."

"And kill people too, right?"

"It'll definitely do that."

"I suspect that you're a violent man, too," she finally said. "And at times I'll bet you're even brutal."

"I'm a lovable cuss when I can be," Fargo assured her. "With me it's live and let live. But at times I do what needs to be done."

"Even killing, right?"

Fargo nodded. "Even killing."

Fargo spent the rest of his third day in the borderland holed up in a clump of juniper trees on the American side of the Rio Grande. It was a good vantage point near Tierra Seca that allowed him to observe anyone riding in or out of the border hovel.

He had nothing but hunches to go on, but based on Carrie's remarks and Rosario Velasquez's odd behavior he suspected that Rosario was linked somehow to the three men trying to kill him. Fargo had decided not to contact Colonel Evans until he could supply more information. After all, the Rio often shifted its course on its own, and unless Fargo could also provide some specific evidence he might be brushed aside.

But the day's long vigil proved fruitless when the trio failed to materialize. At sundown Fargo gave it up as a bad job and returned to the sandy draw where he had spent the previous night. He ate a spartan meal of dried fruit and a handful of parched corn, resolving to ride into El Paso in the morning to stock up on ammo and supplies. At least, for a change, he was flush with cash—three months of generous wages for his services down in Old Mexico along the Camino Real, or King's Highway.

He rode out well before dawn and reached the adobe-pocked hilltops of El Paso just as the sun was rising on the sleepy Southwestern town. Milk and ice wagons rattled along the dusty streets, and Fargo's first stop was the Early Bird Café on Alameda Street. He stoked his hunger-pinched belly with a big plate of eggs and spicy chorizo sausage, cautiously eyeing everyone who entered.

Fargo had felt a scalp-tingling "truth goose" since riding into the city. It was the only real town in this stretch of *la frontera*, and logic told him it was the most likely hub for the imported thugs behind the brazen Mexican land grab. And since he had no real idea what any of them looked like, he was essentially a roving target anywhere in this city.

The readiness is all, he reminded himself as he finished his second cup of coffee sweetened with brown sugar.

A lawman had entered right behind Fargo and silently eaten his breakfast, paying little attention to the Trailsman. But just as Fargo scooted his chair back to leave, the badge-toter spoke up.

"You a drifter, buckskins?"

"More or less," Fargo replied.

"Well, which is it—more or less?"

Fargo gave the deputy marshal a closer size-up. He was a brawny and big-bellied man with the bitter, indrawn look of men who felt that life had somehow given them the go-by—a look Fargo noticed often on the frontier.

The Trailsman knew he had to tread carefully here. El Paso had a reputation for brutal lawmen who tolerated no criminal element in the "better" parts of town, and right now Fargo realized he himself was not exactly the picture of straight-and-narrow rectitude. He was a long way from his last bath, his clothing was dirty and scorched and he was the only man in the café toting a rifle.

"More," Fargo admitted. "You might say I've got jackrabbits in my socks. I just spent three months riding guard for a merchant caravan into Old Mexico."

The deputy pivoted his chair for a better view of Fargo, revealing his massive sidearm in its canvas holster: a Colt

Walker .44, made famous by the Texas Rangers. It was the largest handgun on the frontier, known as the "rifle gun," a percussion-cap weapon with a huge powder load.

"You look like a hard case to me," the starman said coldly. "We got vagrancy laws in El Paso. Can you prove you got any visible means of support?"

"I've got three months' wages on me."

"Yeah, you *say* it's wages. But maybe that only runs lip deep. Maybe it's swag."

Fargo tended to rile cool. This tin star was clearly pushing for a pissing contest that Fargo couldn't afford to enter.

"Tell me," Fargo said, "is Addison Steele still the manager at the Overland depot here in town?"

"What of it?"

"The depot is just around the corner. Why'n't we head over there? Steele can vouch for me. A while back he hired me as a bodyguard for the actress Kathleen Barton."

"Are you telling me your name is Fargo?"

"That would be me."

The lawman studied him. "Yeah. You do look like the sketch I seen in the newspaper. All right, sorry I leaned on you so hard—there's no shadow on your name that I know of. But lookit here, Fargo . . . everybody knows you tend to draw trouble everywhere you go. Mind your pints and quarts while you're in El Paso."

"I'll do my level best," Fargo assured him, heading for the door.

"And visit a bathhouse," the starman called out behind him. "That punk blowing off you could puke a buzzard off a gut wagon."

Keeping his eyes to all sides Fargo rode two streets over to a gun shop he had frequented before. He bought several boxes of shells for both of his weapons and a tin of wiping patches. Then he stopped at a grocery a half block down the street. He stocked up on bacon, jerky, salt, sugar, coffee, airtights of peaches and tomatoes and sacks of cornmeal and flour.

Next he located a barber who also sold hot baths. Fargo scrubbed up and then had his beard artfully trimmed to remove the singed parts. He had just emerged when he was arrested by the sight of a man leaving a saloon across the street.

He was big, barrel-chested, beard-smudged with a mean slash of mouth. Two Army Colts were tied low on his muscular thighs, the heavy model with a metal back-strap. That model had been exported in large numbers to Russia for their military officers.

Fargo couldn't exactly say he recognized the man, but his scalp prickled again—he looked somehow similar to the middle rider in the attack on Fargo yesterday morning, the rider whose horse Fargo had shot out from under him.

Fargo was still sizing up the man when the batwings flew open again and two more men emerged behind him. One carried a bow and wore a fox-skin quiver bristling with arrows. Fargo's face drained cold.

At precisely the same moment that Fargo recognized his enemies, Mean Mouth glanced across the street and spotted him. Fargo was astounded at the blur of speed with which he jerked back both Colts and opened fire.

Fargo's catlike reflexes sent him diving behind a pyramid of melons stacked up on the boardwalk. The hammering racket of gunfire increased as the rifleman, too, began unlimbering. The archer pitched in only moments later, and Fargo found himself once again under a deadly, nerve-racking siege.

Fargo heard a rapid series of dull, hollow *chug* sounds as bullets and arrows pummeled the melons. Pieces of slimy fruit sprayed Fargo as the pyramid began to rapidly crumble under the onslaught. Fargo knew he had only seconds to somehow save his life before he was fully exposed to these ungodly talented and determined killers.

Cursing as pieces of melon clotted his eyes Fargo shucked out his barking iron and risked a peek around the melons. An arrow skewered one of them and stopped with the point only an inch from his left eye. Fargo returned fire, pressed so flat to the boardwalk that he couldn't aim, only point and shoot.

But this was not his place and time to die—Fargo's third slug caught the archer in the hollow just under his left shoulder and sent him into a half spin, howling. His companions grabbed him by each arm and shunted him into a nearby alley.

Fargo lay there amid the mess of mutilated melons for at least twenty seconds, waiting for his balls to descend again. This was the third time now that he had somehow cheated the Reaper, and the hairbreadth escapes were taking their toll on his nerves.

A crowd began to gather, men speaking excitedly in English and Spanish. The Mexican street vendor who owned the melons had been safely off to one side, but now he began to gesture angrily at Fargo.

"Mis melones! Ay, dios! Quien va a pagarme?"

"I'll pay for the damn things," Fargo groused even though he hadn't been the one who shot them to a pulp. Anything to avoid dragging the law into this. He slowly pushed to his feet. *"Cuanto cuesta?"*

"Cinco dolares!"

"Five dollars! *Vaya, hombre!* That's highway robbery. You sell them for ten cents apiece and there's no more than twenty ruined."

"Pay the man, Fargo," said a familiar voice behind him. Fargo turned to confront the same deputy who had just rousted him in the café. "See what I mean? You're trouble on two sticks."

"I didn't start this," Fargo protested. "I just stepped out of the barbershop when three men across the street tried to cut me down."

The deputy looked at the florid-faced vendor. "How 'bout it, Manuel? *Que pasa aqui?*"

The vendor held his silence, extending one open hand toward Fargo. Realizing which way the wind set, Fargo slapped a half eagle into the outstretched palm.

Manuel pocketed the coin and nodded. "This man, he say the truth, *jefe.* I see *todo que pasa.*"

The deputy looked at Fargo again. "Do you know the three men who opened up on you?"

"No," Fargo said truthfully.

"Then why in Sam Hill would they try to kill you?"

Fargo hadn't seen a newspaper and had no idea if the residents of El Paso knew yet about the border land grab at the Rio Grande. Chances were good that they didn't. That stretch of the Rio was remote and a good ride southeast of the city, and given the serpentine loops of the river, only someone very familiar with its course would even notice. And even fewer would believe it was man-made.

So Fargo decided to play this one close to his vest. He preferred that it be the army that first caught wind of this. Otherwise, hotheads south of the border, still smarting from the loss of the war, might provoke hotheads north of the border still smarting from the humiliation at the Alamo.

"Why?" Fargo shrugged. "Maybe they mistook me for somebody they've got a grudge against."

The deputy grunted. "Mistook you? It's more likely some of the no doubt hundreds of jaspers who have an ax to grind with you."

"Distinct possibility," Fargo agreed, swiping a gobbet of melon off his shirt.

The lawman shook his head in disgust. "Well, I'll ask some questions at the saloon. But I'd advise you to dust your hocks out of town. I've got no cause to arrest you—this time. But we got public nuisance laws in El Paso, too, and this just now is about as public a nuisance as I ever seen. *Comprende?*"

"*Comprendo.*"

The deputy started across the street. Fargo unlooped his reins and turned the stirrup, stepping up and over. But as he reined the Ovaro around, he spotted a familiar grinning face watching him from about twenty yards down on Fargo's side of the street.

"Son of a *bitch*," the Trailsman swore under his breath. "That man is becoming my hair shirt."

Santiago Valdez, grinning like the cat who fucked the canary before he ate it, crooked his right index finger at Fargo, beckoning him to join him.

7

Valdez forked leather as Fargo approached him.

"Hope you enjoyed the show," Fargo greeted him. "Maybe I ought to start selling tickets."

"Oh, I enjoyed it. But I fear now that you'll be suffering from *melon*cholia."

Fargo scowled. "My side aches, I'm laughing so hard. Thanks for giving me a hand."

"You didn't need me. Fargo, that was impressive. You're starting to rattle them now. Yesterday you killed one of their horses; just now you wounded one of them. Those three aren't used to effective resistance. You are one tough monkey."

"Could this be love?" Fargo shot back sarcastically. He cast a glance over his shoulder toward the saloon. "Look, let's skedaddle. I'm that law dog's favorite boy now."

"Did he throw you out of town?"

"Not quite. But he's on the feather edge of jugging me."

"There's a saloon on the next street over. I'll stand you to a drink."

The two men reined left at the next cross street and tied off at a corner saloon called La Paloma Blanca. Fargo ordered a beer, Valdez a whiskey, and they sat at a table away from prying ears.

"Don't worry too much about Jim West," Valdez assured him. "He likes to swing his eggs around, but he barks more than he bites. He's not so bad for an El Paso lawman. I've locked horns with him a couple times, too."

"Never mind that," Fargo said after taking a sweeping-deep slug of his beer and knuckling foam off his mustache. "I'm getting sick of this coy schoolgirl shit of yours. You're obviously staying on those three bastards like white on rice. You won't tell

47

me why. All right, that's your beeswax. But a man can only jump over a snake so many times before he finally gets the fangs in his ass. At least tell me where they're holed up."

"Why? So you can kill them and ruin my plans?"

"Look, that's the third time now in four days that they've tried to douse my glims."

"Fargo, I've figured out by now that you're like a cat—which means you've still got six lives left."

Fargo expelled a long sigh of frustration. "Christ, let's not cloud the issue with facts, huh? Since you're bird-dogging them so close, why didn't you follow them when they took off running?"

"Because they're always dangerous, but even more so when the pressure is on. I already told you I'm not after them. I want the son of a bitch whose boots they lick. If I let them kill me—or if I help you kill *them*—I'm up the creek without a paddle."

"All right," Fargo said, "I do plan to kill them. I admit it. What choice do I have except to run away? But just like you I first want to locate the honcho."

Valdez shook his head emphatically. "Just like me? Like hell! *You* want to find the brain behind the muscle so you can report him to the army—you told me so. I intend to kill him. If I cooperate with you, I shoot a hole in my own canoe."

"What's the difference? Either way the head hound will find his dick in the wringer. What he did jeopardizes the U.S. and amounts to treason, which means he'll stretch hemp or face a firing squad."

Valdez's eyes went distant and his face hardened into a mask of pure hate.

"What's the difference? *Vaya*—this son of a bitch plays the government like a piano. Besides, 'treason' is a strange word coming from you, Fargo. Since when do you wrap yourself in flags?"

"I didn't say I'm personally offended. I'm saying that's the federal offense."

"I don't give a shit about any of those words," Valdez said, "and I don't count on the cheese dicks in the government to settle my scores. Do you?"

Fargo's silence answered for him.

Valdez added, "I know it makes no sense to you. Like the philosopher says: The heart has its own reasons, and *reason* cannot understand them."

Fargo studied that hate-twisted face. "I take your point. You want the man who controls these three because, somehow or other, he caused the death of someone you love, right?"

Valdez ignored the question.

"The man you're after," Fargo pressed, "is he at the very top of the heap?"

"For my purposes, yes. For yours, no. He, too, is fed by a master. But I don't care about the top dog either."

"Maybe you haven't noticed how this is personal for me, too. Those three are hell-bent on killing me."

"Yeah, but I was on their list before you were. Their boss made sure of that."

"*Do* you know where they're holed up?"

Again Valdez remained silent. But this time, Fargo noticed hopefully, he seemed to be debating with himself.

"Look, Fargo," he finally replied, "I have a general idea where they are. I also happen to think you're a basically decent man and I don't want to see you cut down. Besides, I could use your help to a point. But before I tell you anything, I'll have to get your word that you won't kill them until I get my man."

Valdez paused to knock back his drink. "More important, if you manage to track them to their boss before I do, I want your solemn oath you won't kill him, either. *That* pig's afterbirth is mine. After I put him under, you can do whatever the hell you want to with my blessing."

"Since I don't give my word lightly, let's chew this a little finer. You saw what happened today—I might have to kill in self-defense."

"You'll never kill all three of them at once—never. What I'm asking is that at least one stays alive. That's my best chance of finding the man I really want."

"Well," Fargo said, "you want to kill their boss and I at least want to know who he is—something you evidently already know—so I can get to the robber baron above him. So I'll give you my word—insofar as I can."

Valdez nodded. "Have you heard of Scorpion Town?"

Fargo nodded. "Sure. It's the roughest part of El Paso.

About five square blocks in the south of the city past the slaughterhouse."

"Yes. Filled with shacks, fleapit boardinghouses, grog shops, cathouses, gambling dens—a place the law seldom enters and never after dark. I've tracked them to the edge of the place, but I always lose them in the twisting, narrow alleys."

"You telling me they take horses into a smoky row like that?"

Valdez shook his head. "They board their horses on the western flank of Scorpion Town, at the livery stable on Paisano Street—place owned by an old man named Benito Gonzalez. But he's crooked as cat shit, and you don't want to ask him no questions."

" 'Preciate the information. I got a pretty good look at all three of them today, so at least I know who to look for."

Valdez spun his empty glass around in his fingers. "I trust your word. But you're the last man I should be helping— you're too damn good at what you do. *Por eso*, you might learn too much and get in my way. That would be unfortunate for you."

"Here we go again, ring-around-the-rosy," Fargo said wearily. "I take it we're back to the thinly veiled threats?"

"I would not threaten a man like you, Fargo. Either I would kill him or I would not. But no threats. I do, however, give fair warning at times if I respect a man."

"Fair enough. As for getting in your way, I won't do it on purpose. And I won't hesitate to kill you either if it comes to that. Let's hope it doesn't. Just one more question."

"Questions don't bother me because it's answers that matter, and I give very few."

"What do you know about Rosario Velasquez back in Tierra Seca?"

Valdez grinned. "What *any* red-blooded man would know the moment he sees her."

"Yeah, she's some looker. But why would she bother to warn me I'm a dead man if I side you? What's it to her?"

Valdez assumed an innocent mien and shrugged. "Can any man read sign on the breast of a woman? Better to ask what came before time began."

"Is she tied in with these three killers somehow?"

"I hear that all women are weak reeds in your hands, Trailsman. Find out for yourself. Bend her to your will after you poke her."

"Once again," Fargo said, "I come up with nothing but the sniffles. Well, what about this commune leader, Ripley Parker? You got any skinny on him?"

"That's two questions, but I'll answer: All I know is that, like you, I don't trust him. But clearly he gets a lot of pussy, and maybe that's all he's after."

"You know," Fargo said, "my life would be a lot simpler right now if I'd left that damn arrow in your leg. Well, maybe I'll see you in hell, huh?"

Fargo clapped on his hat and started to scrape back his chair.

"Speaking of hell," Valdez spoke up, arresting Fargo's movement, "there is one more thing I can tell you because it does not interfere with me. From now on, sleep on your guns."

"I'm doing that already."

"Then do not even sleep. There is a fourth killer, this one coming down from Taos. He is an Apache, and he is the worst hurt in the world. He makes the three you are up against now look like toothless dogs. At first he was summoned only to kill me, but almost certainly you are now a target also."

"An Apache?" Fargo repeated. "There are plenty of dangerous killers in that tribe—what's he called?"

"You won't know his name. Unlike you, he has no reputation. That is because only those who live around him know his name, and they live in terror of repeating it. It is said that he lives by night, the Apache way of saying he practices witchcraft, not religion. Just saying his name, they believe, means certain death because he was spawned from the same evil that created *el* diablo himself."

"As usual with you," Fargo said, frustration clear in his voice, "I ain't got the foggiest notion in hell what you're talking about."

"I told you all you need to know."

"Yeah, well, if all you just said is true, how do you know about him and that he's coming?"

"I make it my job to hear things that I'm not supposed to."

"And you believe everything you hear?"

"Fargo," Valdez said, "everything we have discussed in

this saloon means nothing if you do not believe what I tell you now: The Apache is coming, and hell is coming with him."

Every Coyotero Apache knew the story about Mankiller although few ever spoke of it, and then only in hushed whispers.

It was said that, at the exact moment he was born in the heart of Apacheria, a wild black stallion no one had ever seen before or ever saw again raced past the crude wickiup where his mother gave birth. She was Spanish and Apache, a highly feared *bruja*, or witch, trained in the black arts known as *anti*, the Witchery Way. That wild-eyed black stallion, the people said, was an omen that her son belonged to the evil of night, not to the Coyotero people or even the human race.

Mankiller grew into a mountain of a man, thick-limbed and superbly muscled. His face was like carved granite, never wearing an expression, never registering emotion. His most striking and lethal feature, however, was his huge, powerful hands. Each finger was as thick as a bluecoat picket pin, each raw knuckle like a big stone. They were menacing, dangerous hands—hands capable of choking a bull to death.

And it was these hands that were his weapons of choice. Mankiller's grip was so huge and powerful it could cut off both the jugular and the trachea, stopping blood and air simultaneously. In the Apache world he was unsurpassed in stalking and tracking, unsurpassed at silent movement, cover and concealment. His victims received no warning, no mercy, no justice.

Death was the coin of his realm, a coin he spent freely. No man looked him in the eye, for it was said he had inherited *mal ojo*, the eye of the evil fascinator, from his dam. Mothers hurried their infants from his sight, for any child he fixed his gaze upon soon sickened and died.

Men hated and feared him, yet none ever challenged him, not even the hotheaded white men who killed any Apache foolish enough to roam among them. More than one had pissed his pants in fear when Mankiller cast those lifeless, terrifying eyes upon them.

And now, as he crossed the central plaza of Taos pueblo, the path cleared before him like water before the prow of a ship.

Mankiller lived in an abandoned shack at the edge of the pueblo, and no one knew how he supported himself but he always had money—white man's gold and silver. He had no friends, spoke to no one, and was suspected in the brutal murders of several locals—all strangled to death and found with their broken necks so swollen their chins seemed to have disappeared. But Mankiller was never charged because no man had the courage to try to arrest him.

He crossed the huge plaza slowly, head turning neither left nor right. As he walked he rhythmically squeezed two solid, India rubber balls to keep his hands and wrists strong. At the far side of the plaza he stopped in front of a mud-brick dwelling, still squeezing the balls.

Inside, an old Mexican woman named Maria Santos was stirring a pot of posole. She was known as a *curandero* who mixed herbal potions and gathered medicinal plants in the surrounding valley. It was also believed that she was a soothsayer who possessed the "third eye" that allowed her to see the future.

She had just begun to taste the stew when a shadow fell over the entire doorway, blocking out the sun. Instantly her blood seemed to stop and flow backward in her veins.

"You," she said without turning around. She made the sign of the cross.

Mankiller bent forward to clear the doorway and took one step inside. The voice that spoke to the old woman was guttural and labored, as if badly rusted from lack of use.

"Throw the bones, *vieja.*"

Trembling in every limb, still refusing to look at the visitor, Maria rose from her kneeling position in front of the baked-clay hearth. She reached toward a shelf made of crossed sticks and picked up a wooden box. Inside the box were, among other magical items, a dozen small animal bones, brightly painted in red, black and yellow: the "pointing bones" said to divine future events.

Sweat poured profusely from her face, and her hands trembled so violently that she almost dropped the box. She moved to the center of the rammed earth floor and outlined a circle with evenly spaced animal claws and teeth taken from the box. When she was finished she drew out a silver necklace, from which hung a single charm in the image of a bluebird. This she draped around her neck.

Steadfastly avoiding Mankiller's steady, unblinking gaze,

she dipped a shallow wooden bowl into a pail of water and added a pinch of salt, setting it near the circle of claws and teeth.

Her voice echoed deep and resonant in the silent room.

"Water and salt! Water and salt! Make the bones speak true."

Her scrawny old arm flipped the box upside down and spilled the bones into the circle, scattering them. Mankiller waited, steady and silent as a rock monolith, for a full five minutes as she studied them intently.

"Soon," she finally told him, "you will be summoned to the south country. To *la frontera*."

"To kill?" said the rusted voice.

"Yes, to kill. You will go up against a worthy opponent— a man with eyes the clear blue of a mountain lake. It will be the hardest fight of your life."

"I will kill him?"

Again she studied the bones intently. "The bones will not tell me."

Mankiller took another step into the room. "Throw them again. Make them tell you, or I will kill you."

Soaked in perspiration by now, so frightened that her tongue stuck to the roof of her mouth, Maria gathered up the bones and scattered them again. Again she studied them closely.

"It will be the hardest fight of your life," she finally repeated. "He is a strong man, a cunning man. Terror was his midwife, vengeance his first cry. Killing spawned this man.

"You must attack under a full moon, in the darkest part of the night, at a place where two worlds meet. A lone coyote will howl, and that is when you must strike."

Mankiller took his third step into the room and raised those monstrous hands, dropping the India rubber balls to free his grip. "Only one more time will I say it, dried-up old bitch. Will I kill him?"

Maria forced herself to look at those hands, and the sharp smell of urine filled the room when her bladder emptied itself.

"Before that howl falls silent," she whispered hoarsely, "the blue-eyed one will be dead."

8

Fargo figured he had already called enough attention to himself in El Paso for one day. He decided to let things simmer down there while he returned to Tierra Seca.

Before he left the city he purchased a copy of the *El Paso Beacon* and scoured it for any mention of the sudden channel shifting of the Rio Grande. He was relieved when he discovered nothing, yet he also realized it was only a matter of time before all hell might break loose.

Fargo's main stake in this deal was personal. Three murderous pieces of human garbage were determined to kill him as soon as possible and had already tried three times. Fargo intended to balance that ledger with lead. But every day that passed without exposing this brazen plot increased other dangers.

The mining kingpin who was almost certainly behind this land grab would not likely wait very long before he began exploiting those ridges. Even if Mexican officials had been bribed into silence, Mexico was a hotbed of simmering resentments and peasant armies, and international violence could erupt at any time. The grand scheme of history didn't much concern Fargo. But this mare's nest had been thrust upon him and now he hoped to at least thrust it into the jurisdiction where it properly belonged: the U.S. Army.

Fargo had worked under various contracts with the frontier army, off and on, for many years. He knew that, with the rare exception of battlefield commissions, virtually every officer was a West Point man—and the main subject of study at West Point was combat engineering.

Fargo was confident that if one of these officers studied

the area where the Rio Grande had been rerouted, he would quickly determine that a man-made blast had caused it, not Mother Nature. And a second carefully shaped blast could restore the Rio to its natural course.

However, Fargo was equally convinced that the army would not make such an inspection unless Fargo could give Colonel Evans enough concrete evidence to justify the order. And one key to that evidence, despite the clear threat to Fargo's life, was the borderland roach pit of Tierra Seca.

He rode in late in the afternoon of his fourth day in the border country. The place languished in the furnace heat, the air so hot that each brittle breath felt like molten glass. Again, as a vigilant Fargo trotted the Ovaro into the settlement, he studied the ridges on the Mexican side of the river.

They were almost the exact height and formation as the silver-bearing ridges downstream where the blasting had occurred. Would the greedy kingpin repeat his operation here, too? If so, this time it could be a bloody enterprise— Tierra Seca and the Phalanx commune hugged the American bank of the Rio Grande tightly.

Fargo spotted the beauty Rosario Velasquez the moment he entered the cantina. The place was nearly deserted and she sat at one of the crude tables by herself, braiding her hair.

"*Una copa*, Senor Fargo?" Antonio Two Moons greeted him.

"*Dos copas*," Fargo replied, planking his money.

He carried the two wooden cups of pulque to Rosario's table. "Mind if I join you, pretty lady?"

"*Claro.* I always welcome handsome men. A woman sees very few in *la cola del mundo*."

"You lost me on the Spanish."

"It means 'the tail end of the world.' But that is a polite translation."

Fargo grinned and set a cup in front of her, seating himself only after managing to shoehorn his long legs under the table.

"And a man sees very few beauties like you in these parts," he countered.

Her dangerous eyes turned mischievous for a moment. "Ah? And what about the gringa beauty who calls herself Peace Child? You have seen *all* of her, *verdad*?"

Fargo shrugged. "No secrets around here, huh?"

She flashed her beguiling smile. "Oh, there are many secrets," she assured him. "Most of them very deadly."

"And you know some of them?"

"I know *all* of them. Around me, even the most—how you say?—discreet man becomes an oracle."

Fargo nodded. "Yeah. Beautiful women do that to some men."

"Some men? But not you?"

Fargo ignored the question. "I'm just curious. What the hell is a woman like you doing here?"

"Why, I am a whore, foolish man. What else could I do in a place like this—teach school?"

"If you're a soiled dove, why aren't there men lined up outside this cantina day and night? I've never seen a whore with your beauty."

"*Vaya!* Not that kind of whore. I prefer outlaws with plenty of money, and many such men pass through Tierra Seca. I seduce them one at a time and remain their woman until they no longer have money. Then I select another."

"That sounds like a dangerous game, lady."

"Yes, it is the danger that makes me do it. Do you know that I cannot come unless the man who is bulling me holds a cocked pistol to my head or a knife to my throat?"

"Well, with me it's always the lady's choice. But keep that up and one of these days you'll be going instead of coming."

She laughed that throaty, groin-tickling laugh. "I like you, Fargo. Tell me, would *you* be willing to put a cocked gun to my head for the pleasure of taking me?"

"Nope. But you wouldn't need that with me. I aim to please."

"Oh-*ho*! Is this a challenge?"

"Nah. Just the truth."

"I will be thinking about that," she assured him. "But tell me . . . you must have vast experience with women. What makes a beauty such as this Peace Child simply give it away for no profit?"

Fargo shrugged. "I don't analyze women, Rosario. I just enjoy them. I s'pose the profit, for most women, is the pleasure they get out of it."

"Again you are trying to excite me. And again you have succeeded. Let us go to my house now."

Fargo chuckled. "Lass, I'd love to screw myself into a slight limp with you. But I *don't* like danger during the rut. Just about the time I'd be hitting my high note, your outlaw boyfriend could pop a round into my skull."

Her luscious, full lips formed a pout. "Does this mean I will never put your boasts to the test?"

"I didn't say never. Listen, you just mentioned how men turn into oracles around you. You know, you're sort of an oracle yourself."

"*De veras?* How?"

"The first time I saw you, you warned me I was a dead man if I sided Santiago Valdez. Why?"

She tossed back her head and laughed. "What a stupid question. Because it is the truth, *guapo*."

"Not the whole truth. Whoever the man is who told you that plans to kill me whether I side Valdez or not. You know that, too, don't you?"

"Of course. I know everything. But you are much man, and so far he has failed."

"Not by very much, *querida*. I know your man and his two partners stay in El Paso somewhere. Any idea where?"

"I never ask because I do not care. But even if I did know this, I would not tell you. It is not because I am loyal—I hate the pig and I like you. But I never shape events—I only watch them play out."

"I guess that means you won't tell me any names either."

"*Eres loco?* I should give up a good—how you say?—meal ticket to help you? This pig has given me hundreds of dollars so far. Do you have that kind of money?"

Fargo shook his head. "Not hardly. Well, tell me this: Do they ride into Tierra Seca *only* because you are here? Or do they have some other business here?"

She sent him a sly smile. "I see you are as intelligent as you are handsome. Fargo, perhaps it would be wise of you to talk to Ripley Parker."

"Why?"

"Oh, he has a great interest in you. You should take a greater interest in him."

"I will," Fargo said. "Thanks for the advice."

Fargo finished his drink, bade Rosario good-bye, and headed for the door.

"Fargo!" her voice called out behind him. He turned around.

"Time is a bird," she said, "and the bird is on the wing. Work fast, gringo *famoso*. Work very fast. And watch for what is coming—death is closing in on you now."

Fargo had already found out, from Carrie Stanton, which adobe dwelling Rosario lived in. After sundown he led the Ovaro through the thigh-deep Rio Grande to the Mexican side. He made a cold camp at the base of the long ridge in a spot directly across from Rosario's house.

At least one of the three men trying to kill him was almost certainly coming to see her there, but Fargo couldn't know when. He suspected that Santiago Valdez knew they were meeting there and that he was somehow eavesdropping on them—it would explain his knowledge of such things as the expected arrival of a fourth imported killer.

Fargo's goatskin water bag was running low. He moved a few feet back from the edge of the muddy river and used his collapsible entrenching tool to scoop out a hole in the dirt. Soon it was filled with seep water that was ground filtered and much less muddy than the river.

He drank his fill, topped off his bull's-eye canteen, and then let the Ovaro tank up. He hobbled the stallion and grained him from his hat before settling with his back to the base of the ridge. Fargo gnawed on a hunk of jerky as he began the long vigil of watching Tierra Seca and Rosario's dwelling.

The little settlement was shrouded in darkness and Fargo had only sounds to tell him what was happening. The cantina, sleepy and almost deserted earlier, came to raucous life now that the sun had set.

Someone played an accordion with considerable skill as drunken patrons sang the *ranchero* ballads popular throughout northern Mexico—songs usually featuring a sad, yi-yi-yi-ing Mexican vaquero lamenting the loss of his treacherous woman and his imprisonment in a Texas jail after killing his romantic rival in a knife fight in El Paso or Laredo or Brownsville.

The purling river and the rising-and-falling chorus of

insects lulled Fargo, and he was constantly forced to dip his face into the little pool of water to stay awake. He also spent the time trying to weave the various threads into a tapestry that might give him a larger picture of what he was up against.

Perhaps it would be wise for you to talk to Ripley Parker. He has a great interest in you.

I have a general idea where they are. Have you heard of Scorpion Town?

The Apache is coming, and hell is coming with him.

They're always dangerous, but even more so when the pressure is on.

Watch for what is coming—death is closing in on you now.

"Trailsman," Fargo muttered, "you've opened a can of worms this time."

The Ovaro snorted as if in agreement.

"Nobody asked you, smartass," Fargo said.

For hours, as the moon crept toward its zenith, Fargo focused his frontier-honed hearing on the border settlement. Riders came and went, but none to Rosario's house. To make certain, several times he splashed across the river on foot and crept up to her house. But no horses were tethered outside it and no sounds came from within.

Finally, sometime well after midnight, the cantina fell silent and Fargo settled his head against his saddle to grab some shut-eye.

Tomorrow, he decided before sleep claimed him, he would run yet another risk and venture into Scorpion Town.

9

When the first light of dawn showed in the east Fargo roused himself. He ate a can of peaches for breakfast, tacked the Ovaro and crossed the river, heading northwest toward El Paso.

When the sun was well enough up he broke out his binoculars and rode to the top of a sandy knoll, carefully searching the terrain in all directions for signs of riders. He spotted no movement except a lone Mexican on a burro.

Fargo knew that the three mercenaries were actively looking for him, and his hope was to stake out the livery stable Valdez had mentioned, the one on Paisano Street, and spot them as they came for their mounts. There was a slim chance they might report to their handler before leaving El Paso. If Fargo could successfully follow them he might obtain a valuable piece of information for his report to Colonel Evans.

The three men were familiar with his horse, so Fargo left the Ovaro at a livery on the eastern outskirts of El Paso and entered the town on foot, trying as much as possible to obscure himself in shadows and among knots of pedestrians. When he reached Paisano Street, on the edge of Scorpion Town, he took up a spot behind a pile of empty hogsheads in front of a warehouse.

For the first hour or so he spotted little activity around the livery. A few men arrived to pick up their horses, and a young *mozo* with a wheelbarrow came outside to shovel up manure in the paddock.

"Hey!" shouted a voice behind Fargo. "The hell you up to there, mister?"

Fargo turned to watch a burly worker in twill coveralls

crossing toward him from the warehouse. He carried a sledgehammer.

"Looks to me like you're planning to steal a horse," the worker challenged him as he drew up close to Fargo, lifting the sledge menacingly.

After his run-in with Deputy Jim West yesterday, Fargo was in the mood to avoid more trouble.

"I'm not out to steal a horse," Fargo replied. "I'm hoping to recover one. I was eating breakfast yesterday when three men made off with my mount. I'm hoping to spot it."

The worker had a bull neck and a beefy, belligerent face. But he carefully noted Fargo's two firearms and the wicked-looking Arkansas toothpick protruding from his boot.

"Did you report the theft?" Bull Neck demanded.

"Sure did, to Deputy Jim West. He's the one suggested I keep my eye on this place. He told me plenty of stolen horses are bought and sold here."

This reply seemed to mollify the worker, who lowered the sledge. "That's the straight, mister. Some shifty fuckin' greaser named Gonzalez owns the place. All these beaners are lazy criminals. I had my way, we'd run every last one of them back to Mexico. Was it Mexers who boosted your horse?"

"White men," Fargo replied. "One was skinny as a bean-pole and one carried a bow and wore a quiver of arrows. And one of 'em wore two tied-down guns."

"Hell! I see them there priddy near every day. Matter fact, they come for their horses not long before you got here. What's your horse look like?"

"Sixteen-hand chestnut," Fargo lied, "with a black mane and tail."

"I didn't see no horse like that."

"Did you see which direction they headed?"

"Didn't pay no attention. But they must be staying in Scorpion Town—that's the direction they always come from."

" 'Preciate the information," Fargo said.

"Mister, I'd think twice before I waltzed into that hell-hole. There's pepper guts in Scorpion Town what'll cut your throat just to ease the boredom."

The worker's eyes raked over Fargo. "Then again, you

look like you can take care of yourself. Look, if you kill a greaser, stop by and let me know, wouldja? Me and the boys will celebrate."

Fargo headed across wide, dusty, wheel-rutted Paisano Street. He had learned little from the worker except the fact that the trio had already come for their horses. But he might strike a lode and find somebody who knew where they were staying.

However, his little talk with Bull Neck just now had served as a reminder of the widespread hatred along the border between gringos and Mexicans. If this Mexican land grab became public knowledge, there could be an explosion more forceful than the one that had rerouted the Rio Grande.

Fargo had never set foot in Scorpion Town before today. But it instantly reminded him of other rough tenderloins he knew of including the Barbary Coast in San Francisco and a lawless patch on the edge of Tucson known as Across the River. The stench of filth and garbage was overpowering, laced with the strong, sweet odor emanating from numerous opium dens.

Rough customers abounded. Hooded eyes watched him from the warren of dark alleys that had replaced the streets. Within ten minutes Fargo had witnessed a knife fight and a mugging and fended off countless scraggly soiled doves and beggars. However, the denizens of this wretched place knew the broad-shouldered, slim-hipped, well-armed, buckskin-clad, blue-eyed outsider was no easy mark and wisely avoided confronting him.

Fargo concentrated on the grogshops and eating houses, inquiring about the three men. But even when he greased palms, no one could or would cooperate. A man carrying a bow and arrows could hardly go unnoticed, yet the residents of Scorpion Town had evidently developed a selective blindness. Nor could Fargo blame them for their silence—there was no law to protect a man in this godforsaken patch of squalor, and violent retribution was a way of life.

Fargo emerged from yet another filthy hovel after coming up with nothing but a big goose egg.

"*Sssst!* Senor!"

Fargo glanced right at a garbage-strewn entrance to an

alley. A Mexican in filthy, torn clothing and deteriorating rope sandals beckoned him closer.

"I hear you look for three gringos," the man said when Fargo had stepped closer. A livid white scar ran from the corner of his left eye to the hinge of his jaw.

"You hear right. Do you know where they are staying?"

"*Si.* For *un precio* I will show you where."

"And what is that price?"

The man held up five dirty fingers. *"Americano dolares."*

"Five dollars is steep. Describe these men."

In halting English the Mexican gave a fairly detailed description of all three.

"All right," Fargo said, "but I been spreading all that around. How do I know you've actually seen them and know where they stay?"

"Pues, I theenk there is one theeng you did not say, uh? The gringo with the arrows—he go to *el medico* to have bullet take out."

"So far, so good," Fargo said. "Where are they staying?"

"It is no good to tell you, I theenk. The alleys, they have no names. As you see, they are—*como se dice*? They tweest like snakes in sand. Better I show you."

Fargo nodded. "But I warn you now, Sancho—if this is a fox play I'll have your guts for garters."

The Mexican held out his hand. "First *el dinero.*"

Fargo sniffed a rat here. But so far he was just barking at a knot and he felt that time was turning against him. He decided to roll the dice.

He handed the Mexican a gold cartwheel and followed him through a series of dark, filthy alleys that turned Fargo's stomach. They passed an old woman on her knees performing fellatio on a grossly fat man who smelled like a mash vat; a decomposing human body crawling with rats; several young Mexican boys beating and robbing an old man who screamed over and over that he was being castrated by Satan.

Fargo made a mind map of the route as they penetrated deeper and deeper into the vile heart of Scorpion Town. At first Fargo had wondered why three no doubt well-paid killers would choose such an area. Now he understood why. Anyone trying to locate them might well prefer to harrow hell itself. Fargo already regretted his decision to search for them here.

Finally the Mexican entered a short, straight alley and pointed to a door at the end of it.

"That is where they stay," he announced. "*Pero* they are not there now. Each day they leave—*como se dice? Muy temprano.*"

"Very early?"

"*Eso, si.* Very early."

"How do you know all this?" Fargo demanded although all of it fit the few facts he knew.

"*Mi tio*, Salvador, my uncle, he own building. For two dollars, I can open the door."

Fargo handed him two silver dollars. "Open it. And don't ask for any more money."

The Mexican started into the dark alley. Fargo had taken only three steps when he caught a sudden movement in the tail of his left eye. Something struck him from behind with the force of a mule kick. His head seemed to explode in a burst of white light, and Fargo's knees buckled.

Fargo dropped to one knee and almost blacked out. The Henry was snatched from his left hand and he felt his holster lighten as somebody else on his right tugged the Colt out. He knew that if he succumbed to the darkness now enveloping him he would die in the next few seconds.

Summoning deep reserves of strength and will, Fargo jerked the Arkansas toothpick from its boot sheath even as he heard the metallic click of his revolver being cocked. He dropped prone on his right side an eyeblink before the Colt barked only inches away.

Fargo pivoted on his hip and wrapped his legs around one of the assailants, toppling him onto the upturned blade of the toothpick. Heat washed over his hand as the weapon penetrated vitals. But he knew he couldn't let up now because a second attacker had the Henry.

Fargo jerked his knife free and rolled fast, feeling the wind as the second assailant swung the Henry at his head. Fargo leaped to his feet and lunged forward, driving the Arkansas toothpick deep into his assailant's torso and giving it the

"Spanish twist." The man emitted a high-pitched scream of pain and dropped to the ground like a sack of grain, flopping wildly for a few seconds until death closed his account. The leather-wrapped blackjack he had used to sap Fargo was still clutched in his right hand.

All this had taken only seconds. Scar Face started to bolt toward the nearby mouth of the alley, but one of Fargo's long legs managed to hook him and send him sprawling. With lightning speed Fargo pinned him facedown with a knee in his back.

He grabbed a handful of hair and jerked the downed man's head back far enough to slip the toothpick's razor-honed edge in front of his windpipe.

"All right, cockchafer, I just killed two alley rats. You wanna make it three?"

"No, senor, *por dios*, no! *Por favor, no me mata!*"

Fargo pressed the blade tighter. "One more lie out of your filthy sewer of a mouth and I *will* kill you. Are the men I described really staying here?"

"*Si*, senor, yes, yes! *Mi tio* Salvador does own *este edificio*, and the men do stay here. The only lie is that I can open the door."

"I can open it. But you're coming inside with me. You get cute on me one more time, Mexer, and I'll feed your liver to your asshole."

Fargo wiped off the gory blade of his knife on the pant leg of the nearest corpse. Then he sheathed the weapon and stood up to retrieve his firearms. His head throbbed like a Pawnee war drum, and he was unsteady on his feet.

He leveled his Colt on the supine, cowering Mexican.

"All right, get up. And I'm already tickling the trigger, scum bucket, so at least *pretend* you got more brains than a rabbit."

10

Fargo frisked the Mexican and found a cheap knife strapped to his ankle. He easily snapped the blade from the haft merely by holding the knife at an angle while he stepped on the blade.

"If you're going to carry a blade," Fargo remarked sarcastically, "steal something better than a two-bit frog sticker."

Fargo pulled a passe-partout from his possibles bag, a master key more widely known as a bar key. It was slotted and held four sliding bits that fit most of the door locks. It was part of a "detection kit" issued to him by Allan Pinkerton when the famous sleuth hired Fargo for a difficult case in Missouri. Fargo had kept the bar key when he turned the kit back in.

Keeping a close eye on his prisoner, Fargo managed to open the lock with the third bit he tried. The door swung open with a meowing sound.

"You go in first," Fargo ordered, wagging the Colt at him. "Any parlor tricks, chili-pep, and I'll burn you down."

Fargo followed the Mexican into a single room with a bare puncheon floor and a few sticks of crude furnishings. The place smelled of stale sweat and rancid food. Fargo left the door open for illumination.

"Sit there," Fargo said, pointing the Colt's muzzle at a three-legged stool. "Don't move until I tell you to."

He glanced quickly around. Three crude shakedowns covered with stained and rumpled horse blankets sufficed as beds. One corner was cluttered with discarded tin cans and whiskey bottles, flies droning around them, and dirty clothing was scattered on the floor. But the room, like that saddle pocket he had searched a couple of days ago, yielded no clues to the three men's identity or purpose.

Real professionals, thought a frustrated Fargo. And right now they were likely searching for him along the Rio.

"These three men," Fargo said, "do you know any names?"

"No, senor," the Mexican said. "*Lo juro*—I swear it. My *tío*, he ask no questions. These men, they are not *el tipo* to, how you say, make the small talk."

Fargo believed that. He rifled through the pockets of the clothing. Again he found nothing until he checked the front pocket of a pair of sailcloth trousers—long sailcloth trousers that must have belonged to the beanpole. His fingers encountered a small, waterproof gutta-percha pouch.

He opened it, puzzled at first. A residue of tan-colored powder coated the inside. Fargo sniffed it and immediately recognized the acrid, sulfurous smell: cotton powder, the primer material used to detonate the powerful explosive known as guncotton.

Guncotton had been in use, mainly for excavation and mining, since the 1840s. It was obtained by steeping cotton in a strong mixture of nitric and sulfuric acids. Fargo had seen it a few times, usually pressed into slabs that looked more like papier-mâché blocks than cotton. Just a few of them, properly detonated, would have been enough to cause that gargantuan blast that almost sent him to glory four days ago. This cotton powder, an excellent and safe primer, was merely pulverized guncotton.

At least one of the three men knew his way around explosives. Now Fargo had another concrete detail to report to Colonel Evans. But he also needed names, especially of the higher-ups.

The guncotton blocks could have been manufactured right in this room. Were these men done making it? Again Fargo thought about the ridges opposite Tierra Seca, and a squiggle of foreboding moved along his spine.

"Listen up," he told the Mexican. "I ought to kill you right now—you intended to kill me."

"No, senor, not to keel you! Only to—"

"Bottle it, asshole. I warned you about the lies. Just a warning to the not so wise: You know these three men are hard killers, right?"

The Mexican nodded.

"If you're stupid enough to try selling them information about me, they'll pay your asking price, all right. And after you tell them I was in here, they'll kill you deader than last Christmas. They leave no witnesses. *Me entiende?*"

"I understand, senor."

"You made seven dollars off me today, and I'm letting you keep it. That's a week's wages for an honest worker. Count yourself lucky. Now dust."

"Dust, Senor?"

"Scram. Vamoose. *Afuera.*"

The grateful Mexican fled with alacrity. Fargo left right behind him, locking the door again.

Now he knew where the trio was holed up. But did that matter much? Fargo had decided he wasn't suicidal enough to hang around Scorpion Town in the hope he could tail these three to their honcho. And according to Santiago Valdez, they were damn hard men to tail.

Thinking of Valdez made Fargo's skin pimple as he again recalled the last thing Valdez had told him: *The Apache is coming, and hell is coming with him.*

"Gentlemen," Harlan Perry said in his cultivated baritone voice, "are you absolutely certain that neither Valdez nor Fargo followed you here?"

"Sure as sun in the morning," Deuce Ulrick said confidently. "Valdez tried to follow us this morning from the livery, but we split up and he decided to follow me. I shook him off my tail and then hid in the *mercado* watching him try to locate me."

"If you were hidden, and close enough to watch him," Perry said, "why didn't you kill him?"

"Christ! We weren't out in the desert. There were at least a hundred people surrounding me. After that shoot-out in town with Fargo day before yesterday, I figured it was best to lay low."

Perry thought about that and nodded. "Yes, that makes sense. But I must say that you boys have disappointed me lately—and more importantly, Mr. Winslowe. You're not measuring up to your past record."

Ulrick's mean slash of mouth twisted itself even meaner.

"Yeah? Well, we ain't up against tinhorns here. Both those sons of bitches are slicker than cat shit on ice. Maybe you and Mr. Winslowe oughta take a crack at them sometime."

"Settle down, Deuce," Perry said in a placating tone. "Again you have a good point and I'm caught upon it. After all, neither of these two men won his reputation in a card game. But Mankiller should be here soon and that will end it."

"Boss," put in Johnny Jackson, "this is the third time now you've moved since we come to El Paso. What has Valdez got against you that's got you so jumpy?"

Perry, as if buying time, opened a box of his imported cigars and passed them around to his subordinates. He had rented a pleasant little cottage on Mesa Street, a modest neighborhood hardly known for intrigue and derring-do. The room reeked of eucalyptus from its most recent fumigation to treat Perry's chronic congestion.

"Valdez's personal vendetta against me is nothing to the matter at hand, Johnny," he said dismissively. "By the way, how's your shoulder?"

"Ahh, it's stiff. By tomorrow I'll be up to snuff with my bow. One thing's for sure—I owe Fargo one."

"Mankiller will settle that score. I expect his arrival anytime now."

"Arrival *here*?" Slim Robek interjected in his girlish voice and Appalachian twang. "You mean he's staying rightcheer with you?"

Perry paled at the very suggestion.

"Hardly. Mankiller is reminiscent of the infamous Viking Berserkers. They enjoyed killing with such zeal that, after they annihilated their enemy, they sometimes killed each other to prolong the battle. Mankiller is rumored to have killed his own employer on at least one occasion. No . . . as I mentioned at our last meeting, his handler is in this area and he will be our liaison."

"What's a lee-asian?" Slim asked.

"A go-between," Perry explained patiently. "By the way, Slim—do you have enough material for the Tierra Seca blast?"

Slim nodded. "I got enough and exter besides. I whipped up a new batch."

"I hope you're being discreet—*nothing* in your room?"

"Naw. A body won't find squat in that puke hole of ourn 'ceptin' cockroaches. I brung the hull shootin' match out to the desert. I wrapped 'er good in canvas treated with neat's-foot oil and buried it deep."

"Have you had a chance to study the parameters for this second explosion?"

"Parameters? That word's a might far north for me."

Perry smiled as if indulging a slow child. Slim had little formal education, if any at all, but he was a genius around explosives.

"I mean, Slim, have you worked out the best location for the guncotton in order to rechannel the river?"

Slim nodded. "She's all worked out. Is Mr. Winslowe fixin' to name the date?"

"He's already named it," Perry replied. "We have a date certain, and it's soon. But I won't be passing it on to you three until just before the scheduled blast."

"How's come the big hush this time?" Deuce demanded.

Perry leveled his deceptively mild, professorial gaze on Ulrick. "Because, Deuce, you've been indiscreet with women yet again. I know all about the lovely Rosario Velasquez."

At this intelligence all three of his visitors exchanged astounded glances.

"How do you know about her?" Ulrick demanded. "You got a man in Tierra Seca spying on us?"

" 'Spying' is a bit melodramatic, Deuce. Never mind my source. My point is that you tend to become a little too . . . forthcoming when you fall in love."

"*Love?* Hell, all I'm doing is poking her. She's just a whore."

"You said the same thing about that little redhead out in Sacramento. You remember her—the one who went to the district attorney with a startling amount of information about our activities? If the fetching Rosario is truly just a whore, why have you given her nearly two hundred dollars? That kind of money buys a mistress, not a prostitute."

Deuce's mouth twisted but he said nothing.

"At any rate," Perry resumed briskly, "both Mr. Winslowe and I understand matters of the heart. Sometimes a man, entangled in the naked limbs of a tempting siren, inadvertently says things. So our reticence about the date of this next explosion is merely a practical precaution."

"It ain't necessary," Deuce groused.

"Perhaps you're right. Then again, it would be tempting to warn your lady love to clear the area. And then she warns others. But that could incriminate us."

"She ain't in no danger nohow," Slim put in. "Her place won't be nigh enough to the blast. But them silly shits in the burlap bags all sleep in one big building close to it, and most of them will go up."

"Yes," Perry said. "Tragic victims of ruthless Mexican revolutionaries—or so a respected El Paso newspaperman has been handsomely paid to report."

Johnny Jackson laughed and smacked his thigh. "Mr. Perry, you are some pumpkins! That's just the tonic we need."

"Let's not be complacent," Perry warned. "Fargo and Valdez are both out there, each working on his own. Remain vigilant and try to stay apprised of their whereabouts. Mankiller works fast but it will help immensely if he knows where to start."

Fargo wasn't at all surprised, when he emerged from Scorpion Town and crossed Paisano Street, to find Santiago Valdez waiting astride his roan gelding and munching an apple.

"I wanted watermelon," the copper-skinned *mestizo* greeted him, swinging down from the saddle. "But they were all full of bullet holes."

"You should smile when you crack a joke," Fargo replied, "so I'll know when to laugh."

"Any luck in Scorpion Town?"

"An empty hand is no lure for a hawk," Fargo replied.

"All right, I'll bite. What's that mean?"

"You know damn well what it means. You're the big mystery man whose lips are sewed tight. It's tit for tat, pistolero."

"Just tell me if you found their digs."

"I did. But no way in hell could I tell you where. I just know how to get there—not that I plan on going back."

"I'm not interested in their location—I can follow them when they pick up their horses. That is, I can *try*. The bastards shook me off again this morning. What I'm curious about is what's inside their hidey-hole. Did you get in?"

Fargo grinned. "Tit for tat, *mano*, tit for tat."

"I was going to give you an apple, Fargo, but to hell with you."

By now the two men were walking, Valdez leading his horse. He was silent for about thirty seconds, conning this thing over.

"All right, Fargo. You want information for your report to the army. The mining boss who ordered that explosion is named Stanley Winslowe. He's staying at the Del Norte Arms hotel."

"That's more like it," Fargo said. "Unless you just made it up."

"Go slip a couple dollars to a night-shift desk clerk named Juan Alvarez and find out."

"When did you learn this?"

"Yesterday evening. I finally traced the man I'm after to that hotel. But he's always one step ahead of me. Winslowe is still there, but my target has moved again, and now I'm back to trying to locate a sliver in an elephant's ass. I'm hoping you found something that might help me."

"No soap. I got inside their room, all right, with a bar key. But all I did was confirm the type of explosive they're using. These three are careful about not leaving records."

Valdez nodded. "Yeah, I'm not surprised. But at least I know the room is useless to me now and I won't have to risk my hide anymore in Scorpion Town. Were you jumped?"

"Had to kill two sewer rats," Fargo confirmed. "One of them conked me on the cabeza and my head still hurts. Any chance you'll tell me the name of the head hound you're looking for?"

"I'll tell you after I kill him."

Valdez kicked into a stirrup and hoisted himself onto the hurricane deck. "Well, back to the salt mines."

"Hold on," Fargo said. "Look, I already know that Rosario Velasquez has taken up with one of the three jackals trying to kill us. And I've figured out that you've somehow eavesdropped on them. Has Ripley Parker's name come up?"

"You figure out a lot of things, don't you?"

"Not as many as you have."

"I been at it longer," Valdez reminded him. "Anyhow, I can't see how telling you about her will interfere with my plans. No, Parker's name hasn't come up while I was listening. But I don't trust that weasel dick . . . that burlap-bag horseshit ain't his natural gait. He's a criminal and he's in this deal somehow."

"Rosario made a point of suggesting I talk to him."

"Yeah? You'd best be careful about taking any of her suggestions. That little bitch is in it to win it—for herself."

"She makes no secret of that."

"Maybe not. But I'd wager there's one secret she's kept from you." Valdez leaned forward on his saddle horn. "Did she mention that the pond scum she's currently screwing offered her three hundred dollars to lure you into her bed so you can be killed while you're . . . pleasantly distracted?"

"Must have slipped her mind," Fargo said, his tone ironic.

"Of course. Look, Fargo, there's plenty of willing women in that idiotic Phalanx or whatever the hell they call it. I'd avoid topping Rosario if I was you. I know she's a nice piece. But she's dangerous and sick in the head."

"You mean that bit with the cocked gun up to her head being the only way she can come?"

Valdez grinned. "So you've listened in on her too? And you passed up the chance to kill one of the three?"

"I didn't listen in—she told me."

"See it? When women talk up how they act in bed they're just trying to get you all het up. Trailsman, I would avoid her like a smallpox blanket. She's out to make three hundred dollars on your soul."

"I'm confused here," Fargo replied. "First you tell me an Apache, supposedly the best assassin on the frontier, is coming down from Taos to kill you *and* me. Now you tell me her boyfriend is using Rosario as a lure so the trio can kill me."

Valdez took up the reins. "You're confused, all right. Rosario will be the bait, sure. But I *didn't* say the three mercenary pigs will do the killing, did I? And Rosario won't do the killing, either. So you figure out who's left. Here . . ."

He tossed Fargo an apple. Then he clucked to his horse and headed toward the heart of El Paso.

Fargo realized there wasn't much to figure out. Valdez was telling him Rosario would seduce him so the Apache could kill him. But Fargo considered any man a fool who believed he could predict what that treacherous beauty might or might not do.

Danger was pressing in from all sides, but all in all, Fargo figured it hadn't been the worst day. He knew the type of explosive that was used and the name of the kingpin who was stealing Mexican land. But there were four more key names still missing—four names he was certain that Valdez already knew. Fargo wanted those names before he contacted Colonel Evans.

And just maybe, Fargo thought as he hoofed it to the livery where he'd left the Ovaro, the name Ripley Parker would also figure in prominently. Fargo decided it was high time he found out.

11

The afternoon was well advanced, and Fargo halfway back to Tierra Seca, when he realized he was being followed.

Followed, he quickly determined, but this time not pursued.

It was the same three killers who'd been after him almost from the time he'd arrived in the borderland. Because of a healthy respect for them, Fargo had gone into full defensive mode while crossing the arid flats of the desert. Every few miles he had dismounted to feel the ground lightly with three fingertips.

The desert hardpan just under the loose sand was an excellent conductor of vibrations, and about ten miles southeast of El Paso he detected riders moving at a pace he estimated was a canter.

Following his clear tracks, Fargo guessed, but obviously not interested in running him to ground. Maybe by now he had earned their respect and caution just as they had earned his.

Or maybe they were now under orders to just monitor his whereabouts until a killer surpassing all others arrived to close Fargo's account for good.

It wasn't Fargo's way to passively meet his fate, but rather, to take the bull by the horns and throw him. He mounted and heeled the Ovaro forward toward a dune straight ahead. He rode over the dune until the Ovaro was out of sight on the far side then hobbled the stallion. He slid his Henry from its saddle scabbard and, backsliding often in the loose sand, walked to the top and took up a prone position just behind the crest.

Fargo had also brought two long, pointed sticks with him. He had learned by now that both the rifleman and the archer were better marksmen than most he encountered. He wanted as much distance as possible between himself and them before he busted his first cap.

Fargo planted both sticks deep into the sand at angles forming an X. Then he laid the Henry's long, octagonal barrel into the crotch formed by the two sticks. His sights were normally set at two hundred yards, optimal for game. He adjusted the mechanism to four hundred yards and settled under the broiling sun to wait.

Fargo had decided to make the deadly archer his first target. He had wounded him already, but he doubted that a hit in the hollow below his left shoulder would put him out of action for long. And those sheet-metal arrow points intimidated Fargo more than a bullet did.

When the deadly trio first barely appeared to his view they were like a shimmering, insubstantial heat mirage and looked like one object. As they advanced, the single blur separated into three horsebackers. Fargo waited patiently until they were close enough to make out the coloring of their horses.

BRASS, he reminded himself.

Breathe. He took in a long breath and expelled it slowly, pacing its release through the rest of his shot.

Relax. He willed the tension from his muscles to avoid bucking the rifle. The slightest twitch at this distance would ruin the shot.

Aim. He dropped the notch sight on the archer's face and then lifted it slightly to adjust for bullet drift.

Slack. Fargo gradually took up the free play in the trigger until he met the resistance of the sear.

S-q-u-e-e-z-e, slow and steady until the Henry kicked hard into his shoulder.

The archer's face was suddenly replaced by a red smear. He slacked sideways out of the saddle, his left foot hanging up in the stirrup. His startled horse bolted off to the west, its dead rider dragging and flopping like a sack of rags.

Reacting quickly, the other two men reined their mounts around and reversed their dust. Their experience showed in the way they rode zigzagging avoidance patterns as they escaped, making it impossible for Fargo to stay on bead. Nonetheless, he tossed a few chasers to let them know they were in his thoughts.

Fargo tugged the sticks loose and trudged back down through the loose sand to his horse. The kill made it more likely the two survivors would think twice before tailing him again.

But the simple fact that they *were* tailing him now, avoiding their confident, aggressive attacks, struck him as a troubling omen. That Apache killer is either here, he told himself, or getting close. One question nagged Fargo now: Was the killer everything he was cracked up to be?

Then again, he decided, it didn't really matter. No matter how good he was, Fargo had to make sure the Trailsman was better.

Night was descending by the time Fargo returned to Tierra Seca. Last night's vigil watching Rosario's house had deprived him of sleep, so Fargo decided to make a cold camp and turn in earlier. He bypassed the border settlement.

With an Apache assassin possibly closing in on him, Fargo wanted to leave no trail. He reined the Ovaro into the Rio Grande and moved downstream for a third of a mile. He emerged on the Mexican side and picked a spot within a clump of cottonwood trees.

He stripped the leather from the Ovaro and rubbed him down good with an old feed sack before putting a short ground tether on him and graining the stallion from his hat. Fargo made do with a hunk of jerky before softening bed ground with his knife and turning in early.

Sleep, however, eluded him at first.

The steady chuckle of the Rio Grande, only about a hundred feet away, was lulling as was the steady hum of insects. He also knew that the Ovaro was an excellent nocturnal sentry. But no tribe, except possibly the Comanche, was as skilled at nighttime movement and infiltration as the Apache.

Most tribes had a taboo against leaving their camp circle after dark, but an Apache was in his element after sundown. Fargo had known them to snatch wives from their blankets without waking their husbands. During these silent raids they avoided firearms and killed with rocks wrapped in rawhide.

All this stampeded through his thoughts and kept him on edge even though he had no idea if the killer was even in this area yet. But Fargo had not survived so long by assuming the best, and he decided to guide all his decisions as if this assassin from Taos had already arrived in the borderland.

According to Santiago Valdez, the *mestizo* pistolero was the original target, not Fargo. Which man would the Apache go after first? Valdez, obviously a man with plenty of survival savvy and iron in his spine, clearly feared this killer—a fact that hardly inspired Fargo's confidence.

The readiness is all, Fargo reminded himself. Fighting skill, superior marksmanship, even limitless courage counted for little or nothing if a man lost the element of surprise. Fargo had to be ready, had to be the master of his fate, not the victim of it.

He finally succumbed to sleep, waking with the first roseate blush of dawn on the eastern horizon. Fargo used driftwood to boil coffee, mixing cornmeal with water and forming it into balls he tossed into the hot ashes to bake. After this spartan meal he tacked the Ovaro and began riding in slow, ever-expanding circles to look for signs of human intrusion.

All he found were the tracks of small animals that had gone to the river during the night to drink. When the sun was well up, already heating the late summer desert air mercilessly, Fargo searched the entire area with his binoculars.

The only signs of life were crows scavenging along the riverbanks and the commune farmers already working their fields. There was no sign of "spiritual leader" Ripley Parker, whom Fargo intended to confront today, but the curvaceous Carrie Stanton had already told him Parker was the one late sleeper in the Phalanx. A man who obviously claimed privileges in this "community of equals."

Fargo trotted his stallion back toward Tierra Seca. As he rode abreast of the bean field on the western edge of the settlement, he spotted Carrie and her pretty, green-eyed blond friend Abigail Bartlett hoeing beans side by side.

"Well, hello there, Skye!" Carrie greeted him in her musical lilt. "Aren't you the early bird?"

Fargo doffed his hat. "Peace Child and Hope . . . two of the prettiest farmers I ever saw."

The welcoming smile on both women's faces turned into troubled frowns as they glanced at each other.

"Never mind those stupid 'rebirth' names," Carrie said. "Abigail and I are getting out of here as soon as we can."

"Trouble in utopia?"

"Plenty of trouble," Abigail said. "And its name is Ripley Parker—a vicious tyrant who has the gall to call himself 'Justice.'"

"What's he up to?"

"It's a mighty long list," Carrie said. "The Phalanx believes in free love. But free love means we women have the right to say no if we don't want to do it with somebody. That pig Parker raped me last night, and he's raped other women in the group."

Carrie slid the burlap sheath off her shoulder to show Fargo a huge bruise the dark purple color of grapes. "This is what I got for trying to resist."

"He hasn't done a lick of work," Abigail fumed, "but he's taking money from our crop sales and keeping it for himself. One of the men, Jim Stacy, tried to express the group's grievances to him. He savagely beat Jim up—knocked three of his teeth out and broke his jaw."

"Why don't the men just jump him as a group?" Fargo asked. "There's plenty of them."

"We don't believe in violence," Carrie replied. "Besides, Parker has a gun. I saw it under his bed when he knocked me to the floor. That's strictly against our rules."

"He's up to something," Abigail said. "We keep horses and wagons to haul our crops into El Paso and to bring back supplies. He keeps taking one of the horses to ride somewhere. He disappears for hours at a time."

"And Skye," Carrie put in, "he keeps badgering me all about you, especially about where you're staying and do I know what you're up to. Why would he care so much about your activities?"

"Good question," Fargo said grimly. "I think I'll go ask him."

Fargo nodded toward the long, low, mud-brick building alongside the Rio Grande. "This humble spiritual advisor sleeps there, right?"

Carrie nodded. "He's got his own little room at the left end where the door is."

"Be careful," Abigail tossed in. "He's a dangerous man. Are you going to kill him?"

Fargo had to grin at the hopeful note in her voice. Evidently "nonviolence" had its limitations even among utopians.

"I'm not planning on it," Fargo replied as he started across the field. "Then again, I tend to believe a woman when she tells me she was raped."

Fargo lifted the latchstring and pushed the plank door open. Sunshine flooded in through the doorway and revealed a dirt-floored room with a wooden bedstead in the middle. Ripley Parker, snoring on his back, lay atop a shuck mattress. Fargo tucked at the knees and peered under the bed, spotting a large-bore, double-barreled horse pistol. He propped his Henry near the door and moved farther inside.

"Drop your cock and grab your socks, Rip," Fargo sang out.

Parker snorted and started awake, rising up on one elbow. "What the . . . ?"

"You're sleeping away the best part of the day," Fargo chided with brisk cheerfulness. "Why, your burlap-wrapped flock out there is hungry for spiritual advice while they work their asses off."

The bright sun stabbing into his eyes made the bully blink irritably. "Oh, it's you, Fargo. Wha'd'ya want?"

Again Fargo noticed how the soft Virginia drawl clashed oddly with the twice-broken nose and lumps of scar tissue around Parker's eyes. His shoulders were knotted with hard muscle and the knuckles of his third finger joints were misshapen.

"I see you're a pugilist," Fargo remarked. "Did you fight for money?"

Parker sat all the way up. Now that he was coming fully awake his eyes took on a wary cast. "Not money except side bets. I was the navy champion back in 'fifty-three."

"I'm duly impressed," Fargo said. "There's some tough bare-knuckle fighters in the navy."

Fargo spotted a shelf on the wall behind the bed. It was empty except for a crude, one-foot-tall carved wooden doll with evil black eyes. It wore the black-feathered costume of a *bruja*.

81

"What are you doing with that kachina?" Fargo asked. "That one's a witchcraft doll. The red aborigines never let white men know anything about their hoodoo magic."

Parker waved the question aside. "Why are you here?" he demanded. "I don't appreciate you waking me up."

"Yeah, I s'pose raping women tuckers a man out."

Parker looked confused—Fargo's tone seemed cheerful, not accusatory.

"I see you talked to Car—I mean, Peace Child. Look, she's just trying to stir up a clash of stags. You know how women are, Fargo. They love to see men fight over them. She's just pissed because I picked some of the other gals before I got around to her."

"Sure," Fargo said, playing along. "Stand these women on their heads naked and they all look like sisters."

Parker grinned. "Ain't it the truth?" The grin slowly melted. "Well, is that why you woke me up?" he added uncertainly.

"Actually," Fargo said, "word's out that you been asking all about me. I just thought I'd pay you a visit to see why."

"I just wondered if you were still around the area. See, I've got a little proposition for you."

"A proposition? Sorry, Rip, old boy. I like girls."

Parker frowned. "Not *that* kind of proposition. Christ, you think I'm a fairy? No, what I mean is . . . why don't you join up with us here?"

"Me, run around in a burlap dress and hoe beans for a living?"

"'Course not. Do you see me hoeing beans? And you wouldn't need to wear the stupid burlap."

Parker's voice grew more conspiratorial. "Fargo, this is a goddamn gold mine, man! These silly gal-boys and free-love sluts have got the best farm in this entire region—you ought to see the profit ledger. And talk about good pussy . . . you've already sampled it. Brother, these horny bitches are aching for real men to pound the spike maul to 'em. The pus-gut 'men' in the Phalanx screw like old men. Anything more would be violence."

"Yeah, you fell into a pretty good deal here," Fargo said. "You know . . . what with their other spiritual leader just suddenly disappearing like he did? I wonder what happened to him?"

Parker shrugged impatiently. "Who cares? His loss was my gain. How 'bout it, Fargo? This pie is big enough to slice two ways."

"Yeah, but why cut me in?" Fargo asked. "You rule the roost here."

"Sure. But even a toothless dog will bite if you kick it hard enough. Some of these men are starting to bitch and grumble—some of the women, too. With the two of us, we'd really have the whip hand. The women are all hot for you, so *they* won't bitch. You could live like a rajah here."

"And besides that," Fargo said, "you'd know exactly where I was. That'd be really handy for Stanley Winslowe's plans."

Fargo watched Parker's face closely as he pronounced the name of Stanley Winslowe. But unless Parker was the world's greatest actor, the only response he registered was puzzlement.

"Who in the hell is Stanley Winslowe?" he demanded.

Maybe, Fargo thought, he was simply wrong in his suspicion that Parker was connected to the Mexican land grab. After all, Parker's "proposition" did make sense from the criminal point of view. But then Fargo reminded himself: Men like Winslowe hid behind their high-paid dirt workers to keep the flies off themselves. If Parker had been hired, it would have been by the same man Santiago Valdez was trying to track down.

Fargo didn't answer Parker's question, and now deep suspicion glittered in those hard, scar-encased eyes. He swung his hairy, muscular legs over the edge of the bed as he sat up, looking ridiculous in his rumpled burlap sheath. Fargo watched him edge his left foot under the bed and hook the horse pistol.

"Safety tip," Parker said in a flat, threatening voice. "Leave now by the door or you'll go out through the wall."

"Safety tip," Fargo replied amiably. "Stick to bullying the weak."

Fargo's right leg shot out in a savage kick, the toe of his boot smashing into Parker's mouth and sending a spray of blood and broken teeth all over the bed. Parker grunted hard and snapped backward, sprawling on his back across the mattress.

Fargo's Colt leaped into his fist and he knelt deep, snatching up Parker's double-barreled horse pistol. While Parker writhed on the bed, moaning in pain, Fargo drew back the twin hammers and used his thumb to flick the percussion caps off the nibs. Then he flipped the weapon into the air, caught it by its long barrel, and brought it down hard on the headboard, snapping off both hammers. He tossed the useless weapon into a corner.

Parker managed to sit back up, his bloody lips already swelling. "You white-livered son of a bitch," he said in a tone blending homicidal fury and abject pain. "Lay that gun aside and prove your manhood *then*."

"Your name's on my dance card," Fargo replied, unbuckling his shell belt and dropping it aside. Two seconds later he dropped the Arkansas toothpick atop it.

Parker surged off the bed like a cannonball, intending to head-butt Fargo. But the Trailsman managed to pivot a half turn, and Parker would have brained himself on the door if he hadn't gotten his hands up at the last moment to stop himself.

He recovered, turned around, and moved in at Fargo, using fancy footwork and holding both fists high in the British boxing style.

Fargo, a frontier brawler with no interest in "scientific fighting," merely stood still with his hands out from his hips, awaiting his chance. Parker was impressive, feinting and ducking, keeping Fargo confused. He suddenly bridged the gap in a blur of speed and stung Fargo hard with a left jab to the sternum.

"How you like them apples?" Parker taunted, following up with a hard right that rocked Fargo back on his heels.

Before Fargo could set his feet, Parker waded in and clocked the Trailsman with a roundhouse right that sent him into a Virginia reel. He teetered, almost lost his balance, then regained it again.

"You know," Fargo said, "for a man wearing a dress, you're pretty handy with your fists. Can you cook, too?"

"You won't be joking," Parker promised, moving in again, "when I finish pounding you to paste."

"You just finished," Fargo replied, sending his left leg out in a sweeping hook that sent Parker onto his ass. Before Parker could push to his feet Fargo gripped his head in a viselike hold, locking it in place while he smashed a bruising right knee into his face and broke his nose for a third time with an audible snap.

Parker fell onto his side howling at the pain. Fargo kicked him with savage ferocity in the chest, feeling at least one rib snap.

"You lissenup, rapist," Fargo said. "I killed three men yesterday, and I'll be killing more before I move on. These silly shits in this Phalanx may be fools, but they work damn hard and they ain't hurting a soul. You've murdered one of them and you're stealing their money. I'll be back, and if you're still around I'm going to sink an airshaft through your brain. Savvy that?"

When Parker didn't answer, Fargo kicked him again and broke another rib. "I said, savvy that?"

"I savvy," Parker gasped, blood spurting from his nose. "Jesus Christ, Fargo, I savvy!"

As he buckled on his shell belt Fargo's eyes again returned to the shelf and the Indian kachina. He didn't know a hell of a lot about tribal black magic, but he did know that the secrets of the "dark arts" were never revealed to white men. Such an evil fetish as that wooden doll would never be given to any outsider, especially an enemy who could then use the evil magic against them. And Ripley Parker hardly struck Fargo as the Indian-lover type interested in collecting such things.

Interesting, Fargo thought. Mighty damn interesting.

12

When Fargo emerged from the building, he found a nervous Carrie Stanton and Abigail Bartlett waiting nearby.

"My stars and garters!" Carrie said. "It sounded like somebody slaughtered a hog in there! Are you all right, Skye?"

"He got a few good licks in on me," Fargo said. "Seems like my head has taken a helluva beating in the last couple days."

"Well, you didn't kill him," Abigail said. "I can hear him groaning."

"I'm hoping that little visit brought him to Jesus," Fargo said. "At least, as far as the Phalanx is concerned. He's wearing the no-good label, and if he doesn't clear out like I told him to, I advise you folks to close ranks against him. All this peace and love may work back in Massachusetts, but it won't go on the frontier. Haven't you figured out by now that this Danny Dexter fellow he replaced didn't run off?"

"*I* have," Carrie said. "Parker murdered Danny."

Fargo nodded. "You've got a nice farming operation going here. I suggest you folks get shut of the burlap and the spiritual advisors, elect some good, practical leaders, and continue to thrive. Then you two won't have to run away."

"We wish you'd stay," Abigail said. "At least for a time. You'd be a fine leader."

Fargo chuckled. "Sorry. This placid, punkin-butter existence isn't for me. If I stay too long in one place I get holed-up fever." Fargo's eyes swept appreciatively over both beauties. "Not that there aren't certain temptations."

"Where are you going now, Skye?" Carrie asked as Fargo tightened the girth on his saddle.

"Into El Paso to see a man about a river."

The two women exchanged puzzled glances. "Whatever does that mean?" Abigail asked.

For a few moments Fargo gazed past the irrigated fields, past the muddy brown meanders of the Rio Grande, and focused again on those low ridges on the Mexican side. He had no evidence whatsoever that Stanley Winslowe intended to grab them just as he had the ones a few miles upstream.

But if not, why was his blast team still roosting in El Paso—along with the rainmaker Valdez was trying to hunt down? Perhaps to kill the Trailsman, but Fargo had a gut hunch it had to be more than that. If Fargo's hunch was right, a second blast would destroy the irrigation system that made possible this farmland in the middle of parched desert. It could even destroy many of the farmers themselves.

"I don't rightly know *what* I mean," he admitted. "But I'm working at finding out, and when I do I'll enlighten you."

"Are you too busy," Abigail said coquettishly, "to stay around just a little bit longer? Carrie showed you the cornfield. Now it's my turn."

Fargo grinned. "Well, I did just suggest that you get shut of the burlap, didn't I?"

Abigail took his hand and led him toward the corn, Fargo leading the Ovaro.

"Have fun, Abby," Carrie called out behind them. "I certainly did."

"Skye," Abigail said, her voice rising an octave in her gathering excitement, "Carrie told me about the size on you. I can't wait to see it."

"If you're trying to make me walk funny," Fargo replied, "you just succeeded. You've got J. Henry mighty angry all of a sudden."

"I'll calm him down real quick," she promised, tugging him even faster.

They entered the tall rows of corn and Fargo hobbled the Ovaro.

"I'll show you mine," Abigail said in a voice just above a whisper, "if you'll show me yours."

It took her only a second to whip the burlap sheath over her blond-curled head. Although she was slim and fine-boned, her tits were surprisingly hefty. The fine gold thatch above her slit looked almost exactly like the corn silk all around them.

"Pretty as four aces," Fargo remarked.

"Now you," she demanded.

Fargo grounded the Henry and dropped his shell belt, then his trousers, eliciting an admiring gasp from Abigail.

"I figured Carrie was exaggerating," she said in a breathless voice. "I've got to put that big thing in my mouth—as much of it as I can, anyhow."

She dropped to her knees, gripped Fargo's shaft to control its powerful leaping, and took him into the wet heat of her mouth. She began by rapidly swirling her tongue around the sensitive glans, shooting powerful currents of pleasure deep into his groin.

When she had Fargo groaning, she upped the ante, beginning to plunge him deep into her mouth as she raked the underside with her eyeteeth. She pumped her fist on the part she couldn't fit into her mouth, all the time grinding her tits into his thighs. Fargo felt the strength starting to sap from his legs as surges of hot, tickling, ever-increasing pleasure took over his body.

Her expert ministrations soon had Fargo on the threshold, and she began to whimper with uncontained excitement when she felt him swell to an iron hardness in her mouth. Now her head moved quickly back and forth like a steam-driven piston, a rapid blond blur, and Fargo was forced to brace himself on her slim shoulders when his explosive release drained the last strength from his legs.

A couple of minutes later, with Fargo just returning to normal breathing, she felt between his legs and exclaimed, "My lands! You still have a big old boner! Let's not waste it."

"Let's not," Fargo agreed, pushing her down gently onto her back and separating her satin-smooth thighs.

Around the middle of the hot, lazy, sun-drenched afternoon Fargo left his stallion at the livery on the eastern approach to El Paso. On high alert he hoofed it to the Del Norte Arms hotel on Paseo Street. It didn't seem likely that an Apache would be foolish enough to venture into the city in broad daylight, but there were still two talented gringos champing at the bit to free Fargo's soul.

He dusted himself off as well as he could and approached the huge mahogany door of the lobby. A doorman in gold-braided livery and a ridiculously tall shako hat stepped into his path.

"One moment . . . *sir*," he said, his tone mocking the last word. "May I see your room key?"

"That would be a nifty trick, general," Fargo replied, "seeing's how I haven't got a room yet."

"I'm sorry. I'll have to see a key."

"May I see yours?" Fargo countered.

"I don't have a room here."

"Well, neither do I," Fargo said, "so that makes us even. Make a hole so I can get by."

The doorman's liver lips compressed in contempt. "The Del Norte Arms is beyond the means of the indigent. You will find some more affordable accommodations along Paisano Street."

Fargo's face hardened. "That monkey suit doesn't impress me. Now stand aside or I'll unscrew your head and shit in it."

The doorman dropped the haughty manner and said in a more reasonable tone, "I can't let you in or I'll be cashiered. And I have a wife and kid to support."

"I definitely don't want to cost you your job," Fargo said truthfully. "Tell me, would you be fired if someone over-powered you and forced his way in?"

"Well, no. But—*unh*!"

Fargo tossed a quick punch that caught him in midsentence, landing it perfectly on the sweet spot. The doorman slumped. Fargo caught him under the arms and lowered him the rest of the way to the ground. He entered the marble-floored lobby, well-dressed patrons goggling at sight of this hard, buckskin-clad frontiersman invading their inner sanctum of opulence.

Fargo crossed to the black slate front desk. A fashionably dressed clerk watched him with a mixed expression of dis-dain and fear.

"Which room is Stanley Winslowe in?" Fargo demanded.

"I'm not allowed to give out that information . . . sir."

Fargo expelled a weary sigh. "Here we go again with the

sirs. Look, Gertrude, I've got a knife with a twelve-inch blade tucked into my boot. Would you like to see it?"

"No, sir, I would not."

"I don't like to chew my cabbage twice. Just answer my question and we'll forget about the knife."

"I can't . . . that is . . ."

Fargo began to stoop.

"Mr. Stanley Winslowe is in the Lone Star Suite on the fifth floor," the clerk hastened to say. "But you're wasting your time. El Paso deputies guard his door at all hours."

Fargo definitely didn't welcome that news. Pushing around soft-handed boardwalkers was one thing. But he wasn't about to try bluffing any Texas lawman. He had come this far, however, and decided to play this hand through.

"Sir?" The clerk pointed to a sign on the wall behind him: ALL GUESTS AND VISITORS MUST CHECK THEIR WEAPONS AT THE DESK.

"I can't read," Fargo said, striding toward the stairwell. When he emerged into the thickly carpeted fifth floor hallway he groaned inwardly.

Deputy Sheriff Jim West sat on a ladder-back chair outside the door of the suite. The moment he saw Fargo approaching, he drew his intimidating Colt Walker pistol.

"Well goddamn well," he greeted Fargo. "The bad penny turns up again. The hell are you sniffing around here for, Fargo? I thought I told you to light a shuck out of El Paso."

"Actually," Fargo corrected him, "you only *advised* me to leave. I'm here to pay my respects to Mr. Winslowe."

"Toting all that iron? More likely you're here to kill him, huh?"

"Me, I'm a lovable cuss. This is a friendly visit."

"Yeah, I saw your *lovable* nature in action three days ago when you turned Magoffin Avenue into a shooting gallery."

"I only fired in self-defense, Deputy."

"All right, I'll give you that much. But for such a lovable son of a bitch, you sure seem to have a shitload of enemies. G'wan, beat it. Winslowe wouldn't give you the sweat off his balls, assuming he has any."

"This is pretty cozy," Fargo said. "City law officers serving as private lapdogs for King Silver. I guess he's bought off everybody."

West's jaw muscles bunched tight. "Keep that snappy patter going and you'll be picking lead out of your liver. This is a *private* detail, Fargo, not city time. I get ten dollars a shift for sitting on my prat and counting roses on the wallpaper. You know how much a deputy earns every month?"

"About thirty dollars give or take a bribe."

"You got it in one, bright boy. Plus a dollar for every puking drunk I haul off to the calaboose. Look, drifter, what the hell business could you have with a big muckety like Winslowe?"

"Just tell him Skye Fargo wants to see him for a few minutes."

"Would you like to send in your card?" West said in a tone laced with sarcasm.

"Just tell him I'm here to see him about a wandering river."

"A wandering—?" West narrowed his eyes, scrutinizing Fargo. "Tell me . . . do you smoke it or take it with a spoon?"

"About a wandering river," Fargo repeated.

West heaved his big bulk out of the chair and tapped out "shave and a haircut" on the door before disappearing inside. In less than a minute he came back into the hallway, studying Fargo curiously.

"I'll be damned," he said. "His Nibs said to go on in. But pile all your weapons out here. And the door will be wide open. You try to pull any sneaky shit and I'll blast you into the middle of next week."

"I'll be a good boy," Fargo promised, piling his weapons on the floor.

He entered a huge, luxurious room replete with heavy teak furniture and plaster busts of great American capitalists. A portly, balding man wearing a suit with satin facings on the lapels stood waiting in front of French doors leading to a balcony.

"Mr. Fargo, I'm a very busy man and my time is money. Now, what is this nonsense about a wandering river?"

"Let's skip the parsley," Fargo replied, "and get right to the meat. Are you planning another blast at Tierra Seca?"

Winslowe wore a monocle dangling on a gold chain. He

raised it to his right eye and studied Fargo as if he were a curious specimen of insect. "Are you daft, man? I haven't the slightest idea what you're talking about."

"There's no virgins at this party, Winslowe. I just want to know if you plan on stealing more of Mexico."

"I've heard of you, Fargo. A womanizing drifter whose exploits are ballyhooed in the newspapers and penny press. Perhaps that cheap reputation of yours has gone to your head. To me, however, you're just one more stinking part of the steaming dungheap. Were I you, I would clear out of these parts at once."

"You mean before the Apache finds me?"

Winslowe flinched as if he'd been slapped. "How do you—?"

He caught himself in the nick of time. Fargo grinned. "You just can't get decent help nowadays. I know you'll never go to jail, Winslowe, not with your money. But I'm going to make sure you never pull any of that silver out."

"Ahh . . . now casements are flung open. So this is a shakedown? All right, I'll play along. How much are you demanding?"

"Two million dollars and a night in bed with your wife," Fargo answered promptly. "If the butler doesn't mind giving her up for a night."

Winslowe's face turned beet red. "You arrogant mudsill. Do you realize that for a thousand dollars I can have that deputy in the hallway shoot you dead right now and claim you attacked me?"

"Let's ask him," Fargo suggested. He raised his voice. "Hey, West? Porky here claims you'll kill me for a thousand dollars. Is that right?"

West, who was watching the two men from out in the hallway, replied in a bored tone, "I'd prob'ly negotiate for a higher fee. But for two bits I'd beat the shit out of you and throw away your buckskins."

"Deputy," Winslowe hastened to say, "that was a libel on me. I told Fargo no such thing."

"Technically," Fargo said cheerfully, "it would be slander."

Winslowe lowered his voice. "Fargo, you obviously have no idea who you're trying to intimidate. If you have a price in mind, name it. If not, vacate these premises."

"I'm leaving," Fargo said. "I have no proof you're planning to seize those ridges at Tierra Seca, just a gut hunch based on my knowledge of greedy bastards like you. If you do blast that section it will almost certainly kill innocent people. And if you do that, I guarandamntee I will hunt you down and kill you."

Rage bloated Winslowe's face. "Deputy West!" he shouted. "This trail tramp just threatened my life!"

Fargo grinned. Mimicking Winslowe's own words from a few moments ago, he called out, "Deputy, I told Winslowe no such thing."

"Fargo," the lawman called into the room, wagging his huge pistol, "you're a bigger pain in the ass than my bleeding hemorrhoids. Clear out of this hotel before I jug you."

"On my way," Fargo called back, never taking his cold, slitted stare off of Winslowe. He lowered his voice. "I meant what I said, you fat little pompous fuck. Call off your explosives team or I'll make damn sure you die like a dog in a ditch."

Harlan Perry answered his door and stared at his visitor, jaw slacking open. Even though he had an appointment with the man, it took him a minute to recognize him.

"Christ Almighty! Was it Valdez or Fargo?"

Ripley Parker, moving stiff as an old man, crossed the threshold of Perry's rented cottage on Mesa Street. His lips and nose were badly bruised and swollen, and only the tape tightly swathing his rib cage allowed him to move.

"Valdez? That 'breed has no interest in me and you know it," he snarled. "So, guess who that leaves."

"He might have an interest in following you," Perry fretted, closing the door to a crack and peering cautiously outside. "So might Fargo."

"They don't even know I'm working for you," Ripley said, gingerly lowering himself into an armchair.

"Obviously you've crossed Fargo somehow. What was it all about?"

"The twats at the commune stirred him up. Gave him an earful 'bout how I supposedly raped them and stole money from their crop fund. He also suspects I killed Dexter, their spineless 'spiritual leader' so I could take over the reins at the farm."

"You did kill Dexter. And the charges of theft and rape are true also, aren't they?"

"What's got into you—religion?"

"I told you," Perry said, "to keep a low profile. It was a perfect setup for watching Tierra Seca. If you hadn't been there watching things, I wouldn't have learned that Deuce Ulrick had taken up with Rosario Velasquez. Can you return to the commune?"

"Sure, if I don't mind Fargo turning me into a sieve."

Perry began wheezing, a sign that he was agitated. "You just had to suck Fargo into this. Tell me the truth, Parker. He suspects you're somehow linked to the river plot, doesn't he?"

"He doesn't actually *suspect*, I don't think. But he did some fishing."

Perry, busy peering past the curtains toward the street, alerted like a hound on point. He spun quickly around. "Fishing? How so?"

"Well, he dropped Winslowe's name to see how I'd react. But I played dumb and he let it go."

Perry stood rooted. "He knows Winslowe's name? That means he got it from Valdez. This is troublesome."

Perry felt the jaws of a powerful trap closing on him. Fargo had just succeeded in killing Johnny Jackson. And though Perry had no proof, Ulrick's report that two dead Mexicans had been found outside their door, gutted like fish, suggested Fargo's handiwork—and almost certainly meant he had entered the trio's room. Now he knew Winslowe's name.

"Just maybe," Ripley suggested, his battered lips forming a grotesque, goading grin, "he knows your name, too."

"If so he didn't get it from Valdez. The *mestizo* wants me all to himself."

"Yeah, I heard something about that. I heard—"

"Never mind what you've heard," Perry snapped. "You're being paid, and very well, to control Mankiller and *that's all*. Is he here yet?"

"I expect him tomorrow. He's got a fast horse and he's a tireless rider."

"Where are you meeting him?"

"Why, right here, boss. You'll be alone with him for a while."

Perry turned white as new gypsum and wheezed audibly. Ripley tossed back his head and laughed with gusto.

"Just shitting you. I'm meeting him at a deserted mine outside Zaragoza. It's a little Mexican border town about fifteen miles south of El Paso."

"Can you make the ride in your condition?"

"Yeah, but you're going to have to let me rest up here first. I got no other place to go."

Perry frowned. "I suppose if it can't be avoided. . . ."

Perry wiped his face with a handkerchief and began nervously pacing. "You *can* control the Apache?"

"How many times we have to go over this?" Ripley complained. "Like I told you, as long as I got that phony kachina and he knows there's good money coming his way, I can tell him who to kill and he'll do it. But I can't tell him who *not* to kill. Once you unleash that big, spooky son of a bitch, he's like a runaway train loaded with black powder."

"Well, it's not a perfect world. *First* he kills Valdez. Do you understand?"

"Valdez!" Ripley exploded, wincing and clutching his ribs. "You cowardly prissy—has your brain come unhinged? *Look* at me! Two busted teeth, two busted ribs, a busted nose . . . Valdez doesn't threaten your boss's Tierra Seca operation. Fargo does."

"Fargo is a serious danger to us all. But he only kills in self-defense. Valdez, in stark contrast, is searching for me night and day, and he's closing in."

"Sounds like you got a problem," Ripley sneered.

"No, you have a problem. Remember, Winslowe is completely removed from the management of this situation. If Valdez kills me, you don't get the rest of your money. And Mankiller rides all the way down here and doesn't get paid, either. Use your imagination on that one. Your little wooden doll might not save you."

Ripley did use his imagination. "You've got a point," he finally said. "All right, it's Valdez first—and then Fargo."

13

Fargo emerged from the Del Norte Arms into the grainy twilight of early evening. The doorman had recovered and watched the buckskin-clad man warily.

"I had my little chat with Winslowe," Fargo told him.

"Yes, sir, somehow I thought you would."

Fargo grinned. "I see you haven't been given the boot."

"No, sir. The desk clerk isn't going to say a word because you . . . ahh, bypassed him, too."

Fargo slapped a half eagle into the surprised man's palm. "I didn't enjoy hitting you, fellow. And don't call me 'sir.' I work for a living."

"Five dollars!" the employee exclaimed, staring at the gold cartwheel. "And I called you indigent."

Actually, Fargo thought, the way he was burning through his last wages, he soon would be.

"Punch me again," the doorman quipped, "and we'll make it an even ten. By the way . . . there's a dangerous-looking character lurking in the shadows across the street and watching the hotel. He's wearing two guns."

Fargo glanced across Paseo Street and spotted Valdez grinning at him.

"That's just my guardian devil," Fargo said wearily, heading across the wide, dusty street.

"I don't know how you did it," Valdez greeted him, "but you must have got in to see Winslowe. Did you kill anybody?"

"Didn't have to. I used my considerable charm."

"Uh-hunh. Just like you charmed Johnny Jackson to death yesterday."

Fargo narrowed his eyes. "You saw *that*, too?"

"No. But I found his body when I was riding into Tierra

Seca. Good work, Fargo. But remember you gave your word that you won't kill all three of them. I still need the survivors so I can find their master."

"Johnny Jackson," Fargo repeated. "First time I've heard the name. Far as me killing the other two, don't hold your breath. They're hard men to kill."

Valdez looked worried. "What happened up there with Winslowe? You're not queering the deal for me, are you?"

"Hell no. I threatened the son of a bitch, but he's not worried. But look here, Valdez. You better get a wiggle on and kill this honcho soon."

"You think I'm standing around with my thumb up my ass? Every time I get a close scent of him, the bastard changes his location. And following those men of his is like trying to bite your own teeth."

"Well, try to put some speed on, hombre. *Mas de prisa,* all right? I'm making my report to Colonel Evans tomorrow, but that's no threat to you. The army is a many-headed beast, and Evans will have to work through all kinds of channels before he gets permission to look into this border deal—*if* he even decides to do it."

"What if he doesn't?"

"Then I wash my hands of it," Fargo said. "I'm only sticking my neck out like this because I was unlucky enough to witness it and I figure it's a big deal. If they don't see it that way, to hell with it."

Valdez shook his head. "I don't believe you. I think you're worried about that bunch at Tierra Seca."

"There's that," Fargo admitted. "I'm more and more convinced that Winslowe plans to pull the same river-jumping shit there."

Fargo explained his encounter earlier that day with Ripley Parker. When he mentioned the kachina, Valdez visibly started.

"Chingame!" he swore. "Fargo, that's it!"

"That's what?"

"Cristo! I knew Parker was up to something, but I didn't connect it. *Que estupido soy!* How could I have been so stupid not to follow him?"

"If you've got a point," Fargo said impatiently, "feel free as all hell to make it."

"This Apache killer . . . he's a big believer in *anti*, Indian witchcraft. That kachina you saw is actually Hopi, but *anti* mixes up stuff from several tribes in this region. Rumor has it that a gringo is the only one who can control the Apache. It's got to be Parker, don't you see? That kachina has got something to do with how he's controlling the killer."

Valdez swore again. "It's Parker I should have followed to find the man I want."

Fargo mulled it and nodded. "Yeah, all that rings right. What would a scummy maggot like Parker want with a wooden hoodoo doll? Unfortunately, you're going to play hell locating him now. After that beat down I gave him this morning, he ain't likely stupid enough to return to the farm."

"Fargo, you're the one with all the hunches—"

"I have to have hunches," Fargo cut in, "since you won't tell me a damn thing."

"Never mind the violin. Do you think the Apache is down here by now?"

"I've already decided to assume he is. That's the best way to be ready."

Valdez glanced nervously around in the gathering darkness. "Same here. An Apache, especially one who follows the Witchery Way, is going to strike at night. Be ready, Fargo. Neither one of us has ever faced a killer like this one."

Mankiller had pounded the buffalo-hide saddle of his coal-black stallion day and night, eating parched corn on horseback and stopping only briefly to spell, feed and water his mount.

Now, as his stallion splashed through the Rio Grande just north of Zaragoza, Mexico, a full moon made the placid water scintillate with glowing pinpoints of color. He glanced up at that large circle of moon, seeming almost near enough to reach out and touch. The prophetic words of the old *curandero*, Maria Santos, sounded inside his head:

You must attack under a full moon, in the darkest part of the night, at a place where two worlds meet. A lone coyote will howl, and that is when you must strike. Before that howl falls silent, the blue-eyed one will be dead.

Mankiller constantly shifted the reins from one hand to the other so that he could use the free hand to continuously squeeze the hard India rubber ball that had honed his grip to that of the jaws of a bear trap. It was said, by some who dared speak of him at all, that Mankiller enjoyed killing. But these fools failed to understand: What others called cold-blooded murder was, to him, a duty, even a sacred obligation.

His mother, a highly feared *bruja* among the Coyotero Apaches, had taught him from his earliest years that life was a disease and the only cure was death. Thus he perceived himself to be a *curandero* much like Maria Santos. Whenever possible he killed with his bare hands because it was more personal, as if he were literally handing those diseased with life into the dark underworld of the blessed cured.

This worthy, blue-eyed opponent Maria had foreseen that he would go up against in *la frontera*—an important man must die importantly, and Mankiller hoped to kill him with his hands.

But sometimes this was not possible, so he also carried an old Italian "dagg" inherited from his Mexican father. The weapon was a short, heavy pistol with a hardwood butt that curved only slightly. Its bell-nosed barrel made it useless beyond twenty paces, but its massive bore would literally tear a man's heart out when fired close in, and Mankiller always killed close in. If silence was preferable and there wasn't time to throttle his victims, they were dispatched with the spiked tomahawk tucked into his sash.

He never made his victims suffer; the killing was always quick. There was no enjoyment, no torture, no guilt even when he killed children. And when he sometimes ate his victims' hearts, it was from respect, not depravity. By eating a worthy man's heart, as he meant to eat the heart of this blue-eyed one, he ingested his courage and skill.

In less than an hour Mankiller had reached the played-out Otero silver mine just outside the small settlement of Zaragoza, not far from the sterile mountains where he had been born. He dismounted and led his tired stallion toward the crumbling headframe. He noticed yellow-orange flickers of light and, as he drew still closer, voices speaking in Spanish.

Two voices, he determined. Mankiller hobbled his mount and drew the spiked tomahawk from his sash, listening to the forces of *anti* that always spoke to him on the night wind, guiding him, reminding him of his mission to cure the disease of life. He moved closer across the moon-bleached sand until he could peer inside while listening.

Two men sat near a small fire sharing a bottle of pulque. They were both rough and disheveled, their clothing filthy rags.

"I am telling you, *mano*," said one wearing a filthy headband, "we should steal burros and canteens and ride to Villa Ahumada. Lupe Benevides is assembling a grand army. They will destroy the government and rule all of Chihuahua. I read it on a paper posted in the village."

"Are you crazy?" scoffed the other man, who wore a ratty straw Sonora hat. "These papers are tricks by the *gobernador* to trap traitors. When we show up to enlist we will be shot dead."

"But there is nothing for us here in Zaragoza, Esteban. Nothing but goats and dried-up old crones."

The man in the headband swigged noisily from the bottle. "True. We will steal the burros and canteens as you suggest. But we will ride south to Guadalupe, which is much closer. I have a cousin there who deals with Comancheros from across the Río Bravo in Tejas. Perhaps he can use us."

Mankiller stepped into the entrance of the mine. He was so huge that he blocked much of the breeze, and the fire suddenly dipped low.

"Who is there?" Esteban demanded, pulling a knife from behind his shirt and squinting as he stared toward the dark entrance. "Speak up! Who is there?"

"I see somebody," Headband said, his voice uncertain. He picked up a rock. "Who is there? Speak up!"

Mankiller stood still and silent, his blood singing with the blessed elation that came just before a cure. Headband hurled the rock hard. It bounced off Mankiller's chest.

"Sacred Virgin!" he exclaimed. "I know I hit him hard, but he is just standing there!"

He picked up another fist-sized rock and cocked back his arm to throw it. Abruptly there was a sharp *chunk* sound as the deadly spike of Mankiller's throwing tomahawk punched through Headband's forehead deep into his brain. A huge gout of blood erupted onto the hard-packed floor of the mine with a heavy splashing sound like a horse pissing on frozen earth.

Esteban watched, mesmerized with terror, as his companion took one jerky step backward, twitched violently, and collapsed dead to the floor, heels scratching.

Mankiller moved in with lightning speed, visible now in the firelight. The remaining Mexican took one good look and dropped his knife.

"No!" he cried out, crossing himself. "In the name of God, *no!*"

He retreated one step, two, then tripped on a rock. Before he could scramble to his feet Mankiller was on him.

The Apache encircled the screaming man's neck with his huge, powerful hands. Instantly the piercing shrieks were reduced to a sucking-drain noise as Mankiller stopped the flow of both blood and air. He squeezed one time, hard, and there was an audible snap like green wood breaking.

Mankiller stood up straight and squeezed even harder as Esteban's flailing feet left the ground, holding him suspended until he went slack, then threw the dead body to the floor of the mine as he might a tamale husk. Placing one foot on the first victim's neck, he jerked hard to remove his tomahawk. He wiped it off on the dead man's shirt and tucked it back into his sash.

Then, as if the two fresh corpses were none of his business, he returned to the entrance of the mine to wait for the powerful white *brujo* named Parker.

By the time Fargo had retrieved the Ovaro and left El Paso behind him, darkness had set in.

The desert cooled quickly after sundown and he welcomed the relief of the nighttime breeze. A bright full moon and an unclouded sky filled with an infinity of stars illuminated the desolate landscape in a blue-white sheen like a painting. The most direct route to Tierra Seca was to follow the Rio Grande, but tonight Fargo opted for indirection.

Instead of riding southeast, he bore due east from the city along a route he had not yet taken. An assassin arriving from outside the area would perforce need some information to narrow the search for him. By now the two surviving thugs holed up in Scorpion Town had a good general idea of Fargo's comings and goings, and a general idea is all an Apache would need to track him down.

Fargo had worked with various Indian scouts and trackers employed by the U.S. Army, and he knew they operated differently from most white trackers. White men picked up a trail and followed it closely, sticking to the signs at hand.

Indians, in contrast, tended to locate a trail and then "think into" it. They considered such factors as terrain and availability of water, then made an informed guess about their quarry's ultimate path and destination. Thus they could race ahead without the slow, laborious process of reading sign that often allowed an enemy to escape.

Be ready, Fargo. Neither one of us has ever faced a killer like this one.

Valdez was savvy and courageous, and Fargo tended to believe his assessment of this killer from Taos. But he had supreme confidence in his own ability, and he also knew that fear could be seriously debilitating. The last thing Fargo intended to do was go into hiding. The best cure for fear was offensive action, and it was Fargo's way to meet a threat, not avoid it.

He finally tugged rein due south and bore toward Tierra Seca. It was true that Fargo had decided to file a telegraphic report tomorrow to Colonel Josiah Evans at Fort Union. He also intended to keep his word and give Santiago Valdez first crack at Stanley Winslowe's ramrod, whoever the hell he was.

But this little fandango in *la frontera* wasn't over. Apache or no, there were still two men roaming the area who had tried repeatedly to kill him, and Fargo meant to point their twenty toes to the sky before he moved on. And Valdez was right: Fargo suspected a second blast was in the works, and too many innocents might be in its lethal radius.

Fargo had already confirmed a fact that pricked at him like a burr in his boot. The exact point where the present course of the Rio Grande was closest to the dry, secondary channel just south of it coincided with the big residence building used by the members of the Phalanx. And that first blast, too, had been placed where the Rio was closest to the secondary channel, obviously to maximize success at making the river jump its natural course.

He topped a low rise and saw the dark mass of Tierra Seca hugging the Rio Grande. Fargo didn't plan to spend any time there, but he had to see if Rosario's latest criminal conquest was down there.

Holding the Ovaro to a walk, he rode in a circle around the perimeter of the settlement feeling like a bull's-eye on a target. As usual Antonio Two Moons's cantina was doing a lively business.

Fargo next headed down the only road, passing the cantina and watching Rosario's house carefully.

Perhaps too carefully. Fargo was caught by surprise when a figure close by suddenly materialized from the shadows on his right, sending his heart into his throat.

14

Fargo grabbed leather even as a silvery tinkle of feminine laughter rang out.

"Do not shoot me, *guapo*, until we have had our use of each other. I have not forgotten your boast that you leave all your women well satisfied."

"Damn, Rosario," Fargo said, holstering his shooter, "don't you know better than to ambush a man like that? I came close to shooting you."

"I told you that I like danger."

"And I told you that I don't."

"Then why do you court it so often?" she teased.

Fargo dismounted and tossed the reins forward. "The hell you doing prowling around in the dark?"

"*You* are the one prowling. I live here. Perhaps I was waiting for you. After all, I have been offered three hundred gringo dollars if I lure you to your death. Do you realize how many pesos that is?"

"Funny," Fargo said, "that you would tell me about it. Last time we talked you told me that you never shape events—you just watch them happen."

"*Como no.* I told the truth. But by now Santiago Valdez has already told you about it, *verdad*?"

"*Verdad*. And both you and him claim he listens outside your house. If that's true, just how would you know he's doing that?"

"Because I know men well. And I know that he is—*como se dice*—driven to find a certain man."

"Do you also know why?" Fargo asked her, not fully accepting her flimsy answer.

"That is no secret to those who live around here. He is from this area, and like you he is *famoso*. He is—I do not know the word in English. A man who hunts criminals for a reward."

"A bounty hunter?" Fargo suggested.

"*Eso, sí*. And a very good one. But for the past months he is not after bounty. He is after only one man, and he does not plan to take him to jail."

There was a rustling sound in the apron of shadows to his left, and Fargo pushed Rosario behind the Ovaro's shoulder, shucking out his Colt again. A moment later a dog, its ribs protruding like barrel staves, emerged into the moonlight and barked at them before trotting across the street.

Rosario gave a teasing laugh. *"Eres muy nervioso, guapo."*

"Just careful, not nervous," Fargo lied, leathering his shooter. "All right, this man he's after—do you know his name?"

"Como no. Of course, just as I know the names of the two men you are looking for tonight. But I do not shape events, remember?"

"Yeah, you should set that to a tune. But at least you could tell me *why* Valdez is after him. I've already guessed there's a woman in the mix."

"Not just a woman. A celebrated beauty. Her name was Estrella Marina and she was born in the town of Ascension. Her family opposed her marriage to a *mestizo*, especially one known as a pistolero. But she and Santiago were very much in love and they were married without the blessing of family or church."

A horsebacker trotted his mount in and Fargo watched him tie off in front of the cantina and go inside.

"Santiago was west of here in Agua Prieta when it happened," Rosario resumed. "He killed a man in a gunfight there and was locked in the *carcel*. Soon his wife had no money and she was forced to work as a maid in a hotel in El Paso. She was found shot to death in a—how you say?—a passage of doors . . . ?"

"Hallway?"

"This, yes. She had been raped. A trail of blood led to the room where this man Santiago now seeks was staying. And witnesses heard a shot from his room. But in El Paso the life of a Mexican, even a very pretty girl, is worth less than spider leavings. This man was never arrested."

Fargo asked, "How long ago was she killed?"

"Perhaps three months."

"Three months ago," Fargo mused aloud. "I'd wager he was sent down by Winslowe to make an initial report about the river. But I thought you said Valdez was in jail in Agua Prieta."

"Yes, waiting for his trial. But when he heard the news he escaped somehow. He killed a *policía* while escaping, and the *federales* are searching for him. But Santiago will not rest until he kills this man."

"Can't say as I blame him. And I'll bet *you* know right where the murdering pig is staying, right?"

"No. That is one thing I do not know and cannot find out."

"I don't get it," Fargo said. "You don't shape events, right? So why would you give a damn where he stays?"

"Because perhaps I could sell the information to Valdez."

"Uh-hunh," Fargo said, not sure he believed her. "And that's not all. You've told me you've been offered money to help kill me. You're the one who told me I should look up Ripley Parker. And you warned me about the Apache. All that seems mighty odd for a woman who claims she doesn't take sides."

She laughed. "Never trust or believe a pretty woman, *guapo*. Perhaps I am after all shaping events. But this does not mean they will take a shape you find pleasing."

"Jesus," Fargo muttered. "You are one contrary creature. Look, Rosario, you've just *got* to tell me this much at least: Are Winslowe's men planning to blow up Tierra Seca to shift the course of the Rio?"

"Fargo, I swear by all things holy that I do not know this thing for certain. There are some things the outlaw pig will not talk about to me. But two times now he has suggested that I move to El Paso or somewhere else and do it soon. What does that mean to you?"

Fargo took up the reins and turned the stirrup, forking leather. "I think we *both* know what it means, lady. The clock has been set ticking. And I think you'd best decide pretty damn quick just how much blood you can stand to have on your hands."

Two hours after sunrise Ripley Parker reined in at the entrance of the old Otero silver mine. He gingerly dismounted, wincing at the pain in his ribs. Then he removed a cloth-wrapped object from a saddle pocket.

"Mankiller!" he called out. "It's Parker. I'm coming in."

He stepped slowly inside and saw Mankiller sitting with his back to one of the walls, methodically squeezing the rubber balls he carried with him everywhere.

Enough light penetrated to show the two dead bodies already drawing flies.

"What the hell happened here?" Parker demanded.

"I cure them," Mankiller said in his voice rusted from disuse.

"Yeah, I see that. Make sure you drag them outside before they start to stink."

Mankiller stared at Parker's bruised and battered face. "A powerful *brujo* let some man do this?"

"No man did this to me. I took a bad fall from my horse."

Mankiller said nothing to this, staring at the wrapped object in Parker's hand. Something akin to apprehension showed in the granite-slab face.

"You know what this is?" Parker said.

Mankiller averted his eyes and nodded once.

"With this kachina, whose name is Blood Clot Man," Parker said, "I can pray a believer into the ground. But those who do not believe in *anti* are beyond Blood Clot Man's power. That is why I sent for you—Blood Clot Man demanded it. *You* are a believer, and you are wise not to disobey him. You understand?"

Again Mankiller nodded.

"You will kill two men," Parker said. "Both of them are dangerous. First you will kill Santiago Valdez. Then you will kill Skye Fargo."

"Fargo . . . the blue-eyed one?"

Parker looked surprised. "How do you know that?"

"It was foretold in Taos by the pointing bones."

"Anyway," Parker said, "I have made a plan to trap Valdez. He is a skilled gunman but also a fool ruled by his heart, and such men are easier to kill. But Fargo will be more difficult to locate. I will show you the places where he might be found. And two men have been watching him. I will speak with them about where he might be."

"I find him. Then cure him. But I cure no man unless is night."

"That's best," Parker agreed. "Both the Mexicans and the Americans hate Apaches. You don't want to be seen."

Mankiller continued to squeeze the India rubber balls in silence, keeping his eyes averted from Blood Clot Man.

After speaking with Rosario, Fargo had ridden north from Tierra Seca and the Rio Grande. He was acutely aware that the Apache killer might already be on his trail. He made a cold camp in a stretch of open desert pan and lay awake for hours. He relied on the full moon and the Ovaro, whose keen senses of hearing and smell almost always alerted Fargo to danger after nightfall.

Fargo didn't actually sleep that night. Over the years he had developed what he called the "waking doze" for periods of extreme danger. He slowed his breathing, relaxed his muscles, and cleared his mind of all unnecessary thought, allowing him to rest his tired body while keeping his senses partially attuned. It wasn't as restful as sleep and couldn't be kept up for more than two or three nights without risking exhaustion and carelessness. But more than once it had saved his life.

At sunrise on his seventh day in *la frontera* Fargo rose, stretched out the night kinks, and made a careful survey all around him with his binoculars. The fact that he saw nothing did not reassure him. Apaches were superb at finding cover where none seemed to exist, and their patience, when closing in on their prey, was legendary.

He watered and grained the Ovaro, then tacked the stallion, skipping his coffee and munching on a few stale corn dodgers as he rode. He bore west toward El Paso, constantly vigilant for the ever-expected attack. Although Apaches favored the night assault, a clever assassin might deliberately violate expectations.

The sun was well up, burning in a cloudless sky, when Fargo tied off at the Western Union telegraph office next to the Overland stage depot. He had already composed a tight but complete report in his mind: the blast he had witnessed, shifting the U.S.-Mexico border and seizing silver-bearing ridges for Stanley Winslowe; the hired killers employed to eliminate him as the only witness; the use of guncotton by an obvious explosives expert who could shape charges; and his confrontation with Winslowe, virtually confirming that another blast was imminent, this one endangering civilians because of their strategic location.

There was much that Fargo left out including Valdez's vendetta and the involvement of Ripley Parker. He closed by mentioning that he would check back at Western Union for any response from the fort. Before Fargo left the telegraph office he glanced out the front window to survey the street.

For a moment he glimpsed a tall, whipcord-thin man peering out of the mouth of an alley across the street—peering right at the Western Union office.

Fargo had to decide if the mercenaries were lying in wait to cut him down as he came outside or if they were now spotters keeping tabs on his whereabouts for the killer from Taos. He rolled the dice on the latter and strolled casually out of the office as if unaware of their presence.

"Get ready for a set-to, old warhorse," Fargo remarked quietly as he un-looped the reins and swung up onto the hurricane deck.

He reined around into the street and suddenly thumped the Ovaro with his heels. "Hee-*yah!*"

Fargo shucked out his Colt and headed straight for the mouth of the alley. He had given his word to Valdez that he would try to avoid killing these "bread crumbs" as Valdez called them. But things were vastly different now that a consummate killer had likely arrived, and Fargo was damned if he would just passively let these two set him up for the slaughter.

He charged closer across the wide street, forced to veer hard to avoid an old woman who stepped off the boardwalk to cross. The delay gave the two thugs time to mount. Fargo heard the rataplan of hooves as they fled down the alley.

The Ovaro shot into the alley, ears pinned back, and rapidly put on speed. Fargo spotted the two riders ahead of him, escaping in single file. The burly one brought up the rear, and when he looked over his shoulder Fargo recognized the mean slash of mouth. One of the heavy Colt Army revolvers was suddenly barking in his fist, bullets hornet-buzzing past Fargo's ears.

Fargo returned fire as the Ovaro closed the gap, but hitting a moving target with a handgun from a speeding horse, at this distance, was better suited to a circus trick shooter. And the tight alley with all its obstacles jutting into the way meant Fargo had to control the reins closely, eliminating use of his Henry.

He emptied his Colt and managed to snap the spare cylinder in as the two dirt workers reined into another alley. Fargo hauled back and tugged rein, the skidding Ovaro veering into the alley as the burly gunman opened up with his second Colt Army.

A bullet grazed Fargo's forearm in a searing trace of heat as the two men continued to trade shots. Just ahead of Fargo a huge dray horse, panicked by all the deafening gunshots, reared up and knocked over a pyramid of empty barrels, spilling them across the alley into Fargo's path.

It was too late to rein in. Fargo stretched forward and low over the Ovaro's neck. "Hi-ya!" he shouted. "Hii-*ya*!"

The Ovaro went low and made a powerful leap, muscles uncoiling like powerful springs. Man and beast went airborne, easily clearing the barrels. The Ovaro landed barely missing a stride. Ahead of Fargo the two escaping thugs reined into yet another alley.

Fargo pursued them into it and was just in time to watch them break out onto the desert flats west of El Paso. Now Fargo figured he had the advantage of a stronger, faster horse. He speared the brass-framed Henry from its boot.

Six shots suddenly rang out behind Fargo. They came in such rapid succession that he figured there had to be at least two shooters.

"Rein it in, Fargo!" a familiar voice shouted. "The seventh bullet won't miss!"

He hauled back and reined the Ovaro around. Santiago Valdez sat his roan. He holstered the empty gun and shucked out the second.

"So you'd kill me to keep those two shit stains alive?" Fargo challenged him.

"Kill you? No. But I'll wound you if I have to. Without them I don't find my favorite boy."

"I see those double actions really work," Fargo said. "I couldn't even blink my eyes between shots, they came so fast."

Valdez rode closer. "Now that I've stopped you," he

confessed, "I'll tell you the truth—only one worked. The other jammed on me before I got the first shot out. I told you these things are still experimental."

"And yet you stake your life on 'em?"

"I told you—one always works. I've never had both jam at the same time. That's six shots for me in the same time you only get off three."

Fargo shrugged. "It's your call. I'll wait until they're perfected. So you're still hoping you can follow these two to the honcho? I thought the big idea now is to watch Ripley Parker."

"Unfortunately," Valdez fired back, "a lanky buttinsky named Fargo seems to have driven *him* off, too."

"I talked to Rosario Velasquez last night," Fargo said. "She told me about your wife. Why do I get this hunch that you and Rosario know each other better than you're letting on?"

Valdez ignored his question. "Yeah, I figured she'd flap her gums about it sooner or later. Anyway, it's no big secret. I just don't like talking about it. I intend to *do* something about it—if you'll get off my neck and give me a chance."

"I couldn't likely have killed these two," Fargo pointed out. "They're both dead shots. But I don't want the sons of bitches dogging me like they are. You're the one who warned me to watch my ass with this Apache, and you know damn well those two escaping right now are tracking me to make his job easier."

Valdez nodded. "I don't blame you for not liking it. But the problem is, I think you *can* kill them just like you killed the archer. And I just can't let that happen. It's nothing personal, Fargo."

"Considering that you're making things riskier for me, it sure *feels* personal."

"Things are the way they are," Valdez retorted. "I told you a week ago to just point your bridle out of here."

"Like you said, that ship has sailed. I don't take orders from any man, you included. I'll do what I can to accommodate you, Santiago. But I value my life above your need for revenge, savvy? And there's more lives at stake here than just mine, lives you don't seem to give a shit about."

The two men stared at each other for a full ten seconds.

"Looks like we understand each other," Valdez finally said.

Fargo nodded. "Yeah. Looks like we do."

15

Fargo rode back to Tierra Seca again, taking a circuitous route he had not previously ridden. This time he held the Ovaro to a steady lope, a pace a strong horse could hold, with brief rests in this heat, for hours. It would also force anyone following Fargo to raise dust trails that would show in the clear desert air.

He checked constantly with his binoculars. But the only dust puffs he spotted were well east of him, caused by a bull train heading toward El Paso. By midafternoon Tierra Seca and the Rio Grande hove into view beyond a low ridge.

He rode in a slow circle around the settlement and the outlying patchwork of neat, irrigated fields, a surprising oasis of green in the yellow-brown monotony of desert. Fargo spotted no outward signs of trouble. He surveyed the workers in the biggest bean field until he spotted Carrie Stanton.

He swung down from the saddle and led the Ovaro by the bridle reins out to meet her.

"Parker still around?" he asked her.

She shook her head, smiling at him. "Evidently you persuaded him to take his criminal act on the road. He left yesterday and hasn't been back. He stole one of our best horses, but it's worth the price to be rid of him."

"You know," Fargo mused, thinking out loud more than speaking, "I got a hunch he was ready to vamoose anyway."

"Why do you think so?"

"Listen," Fargo said, "is there some way to call all the workers together?"

She cocked her pretty head curiously. "Of course. But why?"

Fargo gazed toward the nearby river and the ridges just beyond it.

"I just need to say something to all you folks," he said.

Carrie frowned slightly. "Skye, I'll listen to anything you have to say, and so will Abigail. But the rest of them . . . well, you see, one of the reasons the Phalanx came into being was our mistrust of outsiders and their values. The group is especially opposed to violence, and you . . . well . . ."

Fargo laughed. "Yeah, I know. But it was violence that sent Parker packing," he reminded her.

"Yes, Skye, and hallelujah! But most of the others don't know that. Anyway, c'mon. We'll give it a try."

She led Fargo to a clearing beside the big residence building and banged on a triangle mounted in the middle of it. Curious Phalanx members—Fargo estimated around fifty of them—trudged in from the corn, bean and squash fields. Many of the women smiled at Fargo; most of the men didn't.

"This is Skye Fargo," Carrie called out to the rest although by now they knew who he was. "He'd like to address all of us."

"Outsiders have no place here," objected a frowning young man with a wispy red beard who immediately struck Fargo as an overgrown spoiled brat. "This man wears a gun and a knife, and there's another gun sticking out of his saddle."

"That's a rifle, not a gun," Fargo corrected him.

"A distinction without a difference, sir. Both are used to kill."

Here we go again with the "sir" shit, Fargo thought. Out loud he said, "Never mind my weapons. It's *violence* I'm here to help you avoid."

Fargo spent the next few minutes detailing all of it: How he had witnessed, and been caught in, the initial blast seven days ago; the purpose for shifting the river's course; Parker's likely place in all of it; and his conviction that Winslowe intended to pull the same stunt here at Tierra Seca. He added that the blast could come at any time now, almost certainly in the dead of night.

"It's pointless to take all this to authorities in El Paso," Fargo concluded. "Winslowe is wealthy, and men like him use money like manure—they spread it around. By now he's paid off important men on both sides of the border."

The reaction among the listeners was mixed. They had a dim view of rich capitalists, and some appeared ready to believe him. A larger number, however, looked skeptical or even openly suspicious of him. Red Beard spoke up again.

"We don't even know who you are. Maybe this Stanley Winslowe, if he even exists, is using you and this story to drive us out."

"You're so full of shit your feet are sliding," Fargo said bluntly. "Did I say you should leave your farm? All you really need to do to protect your lives is sleep on the far edge of your fields, the side away from the river. It's this building that's in the danger zone."

"Sleep on the ground?" protested a man with jug ears. "You may be used to that, but we aren't. And our kitchen and food and other supplies are in this building."

"So? It's safe during the day, so go ahead and use it. You can see the river clearly from here, and if anybody was down there planting explosives in daylight you'd see it. As for sleeping on the ground, it's comfortable enough if you do it right."

"Such a blast as you describe," said a woman who appeared older than most others in the Phalanx, "would destroy our irrigation system."

"It would for a fact," Fargo replied, "or at least the part of it close to the river. The big problem, though, would be the rerouting of the river. A fancy irrigation system is worthless without a good source of water. But I'm going to be working to stop that blast."

"It's all utterly fantastic," Red Beard opined. "You can't just control rivers like that."

"Skye isn't a liar!" Abigail spoke up hotly. "He told you he witnessed it a week ago."

"And he was *in* that blast," Carrie pitched in. "I saw him right after it happened. His face was blistered and his beard singed. His beard is fixed now, but look at him . . . his buckskins are burned, and you can still see where his eyebrows were singed."

"Naturally Peace Child and Hope speak up for him," Red Beard said, his tone tinged with accusation. "They both went off into the cornfield with him."

"So what?" Carrie demanded. "You're just jealous 'cause we won't do it with you."

"It was Skye," Abigail added, "who ran Ripley Parker off yesterday. How many of you regret *that*?"

"I'm glad he's gone," Jug Ears admitted. "But I'm the one who cleaned up all the blood in his room. Yes, Mr. Fargo ran him off, but he used terrible violence to do it. Perhaps . . . just *perhaps* he has even killed him. No one has seen him."

"Think maybe I ate him, too?" Fargo quipped.

All this seemed to embolden Red Beard further. "Mr. Fargo is an outsider, and a very violent one at that. I've read things about him and all the graves left in his wake. Hope and Peace Child are obviously under his spell. They—"

"Oh, go to hell, Sebastian!" Carrie snapped. "You don't have the gumption of a gourd vine!"

"See?" Red Beard exclaimed to the others. "All of you just heard her! She is clearly in violation of our Oath of Universal Peace and Justice that she promised to obey."

"I'm just curious," Fargo told him. "You're swinging your eggs all over the place right now as you pick on women. But where were you and Jug Ears when Ripley Parker was grinding all of you under his heel?"

"At least he was one of us."

"One of you, yet he raped and beat women? He wasn't in violation of your big oath?"

"Well, at least he *took* that oath and joined us. Will you?"

"I don't swear oaths," Fargo replied. "And I don't join groups. I'm what you might call a majority of one."

"Well, we don't reason that way," Jug Ears put in. "Individualism is the bane of the collective good. It leads to greed, war, suffering, violence—"

"Put a sock in it," Fargo cut him off in disgust. "I got no time for your sweet-lavender stump speech. I've done my best to warn you folks, and I told you what I think you need to do. I suggest all of you at least think about what I said. That explosion could come anytime now."

Fargo hooked a stirrup and forked leather. He swept an arm out toward the fertile, flourishing fields.

"You got a nice deal going here. Like I said, I'll do my best to stop this blast. But I've got killers after me, and anyway, you can't always count on others to protect you. Texas is an organized state. Sure. But it's still a damn dangerous place. There's free-ranging Indians around here including Kiowas, Comanches and Apaches—dangerous tribes all."

"The Indians," Red Beard interrupted him, "were all noble savages until the white man—"

"Save it for your memoirs," Fargo said. "And it's not just the tribes. Here on the border there's roving bands of Mexican criminals who call themselves armies. It's a miracle all of you haven't been wiped out by now."

Fargo pulled his rifle from its boot and held it up so all could see it.

"This is a Henry repeating rifle. You load it on Sunday and it fires all week. You can buy them in El Paso. Somebody here has to know how to shoot. I suggest you lay in some of these and learn how to use them. Soldiers are scarce as hen's teeth, and the Texas Rangers are spread too thin to help you. Self-defense isn't violence, and you *need* to defend yourselves."

Fargo booted his weapon, tipped his hat at the group, and gigged the Ovaro toward Tierra Seca's only street.

Toward sundown Deuce Ulrick and Slim Robek met with Harlan Perry at his rented cottage on quiet, unassuming Mesa Street.

Perry, who usually exhibited the calm demeanor of a riverboat gambler, was now visibly on edge. For a full minute after he let the two men inside he anxiously studied the street through a crack between the door and the jamb.

"Relax, boss," Ulrick scoffed. "We shook Valdez and Fargo this morning. They got no idea in hell where you're staying."

Ulrick described Fargo's wild charge against them after the Trailsman left the telegraph office.

"He come at us like a bull outta the chute—mister, I mean bold as a big man's ass! And it was one helluva cartridge session," Ulrick concluded. "We didn't actually see Valdez stop Fargo. But there was six shots lickety-split from one of the 'breed's double actions, and Fargo just quit the chase."

"Hell," Slim threw in, "Valdez might coulda even shot him. We ain't seen hide nor hair of either one since."

"Nah, ain't likely he shot him," Ulrick gainsaid. "Them two been talking chummy for some time now."

Perry removed a handkerchief from the inside pocket of his silk-lined vest and mopped at his sweat-glistening face. Anxiety always worsened his congestion, and now his breathing sounded like a leaky bellows.

"There's only one reason why Valdez would have stopped him," he fretted. "The man is obsessed with killing me, and he knows you two are his best hope of locating me."

Ulrick looked at Slim and winked.

"Yeah, boy," Ulrick said, "that son of a buck wants your balls on a platter, all right. Be a damn shame if me and Slim got a mite careless. Hey?"

Perry flushed red with anger. "Is that a threat or a poor joke?"

"Ahh, just pulling your leg, chief. But that bastard sure is nursing a powerful grudge against you. The *hell* did you do to him?"

Perry moved to a front window and cautiously peered past the curtains. "That doesn't matter now. Any inkling as to what was in Fargo's telegram?"

"Now *there* we hit pay dirt," Ulrick boasted. "I managed to bribe the telegraph operator. Fargo made a report to some colonel named Josiah Evans up at Fort Union. He didn't mention your name or ours, but he named Mr. Winslowe. And the meddling son of a bitch has figured out the whole plan with moving the river. He knows all about Tierra Seca and even the type of explosive we're using."

Perry dropped the curtain and mopped his face again. "It wouldn't have gotten this far if you boys had done your jobs and killed him. You're not being paid top dollar to give reports about how he's outsmarting us."

"Yeah? Tell that to Johnny Jackson's ghost, why'n't you? You're the one who pulled us back after he killed Johnny. And it was you ordered us just to watch and track him."

Perry impatiently waved all of this aside. "Never mind the bickering. I'm not all that worried about the report to the army, anyway. It's true that Josiah Evans is potential trouble—I know from experience that he can't be bribed. But the army is burdened by a strict and clumsy chain of command, and there are some above him who are more . . . reasonable."

"You know more about that shit than I do," Ulrick said. "But if this Evans is a square shooter like you say, might be he'll act on his own, huh?"

"Nothing is carved in stone," Perry conceded. "This river operation is a first for me. But the politics are on our side."

"How so?"

"That first chunk of Mexico we've already seized is now officially American land, and very soon the area around Tierra Seca will be also. Neither the army, Washington City or that cheap whore called public sentiment will favor giving it back to Mexico. After all, what was the war of 'forty-seven but a huge theft of half of Mexico's territory? This is a mere drop in the ocean."

"I s'pose unless the Mexers get pissed enough to go on the warpath over it. You say we'll grab Tierra Seca soon . . . how soon?"

"I've heard from Mr. Winslowe. As soon as the Apache kills Fargo you're to go immediately ahead with the explosion."

"So the Apache is here?" Slim asked.

"He's here," Perry confirmed, "and believes he's under the orders of an evil wooden doll. Parker met him in Zaragoza early this morning. He's on this side of the border now."

"I ain't ezactly so sure," Slim opined in his feminine twang, "that Mankiller will kill Fargo all that easy. Sure, the Apache is some pumpkins—I shit my drawers just looking at him. But Fargo ain't no slouch."

"Fargo is a formidable enemy," Perry conceded. "However, no man born of woman can best Mankiller."

"He gets *my* money," Ulrick agreed. "But one of these days that cocky Parker is going to lose control of him, and I sure-god hope I ain't around when he does."

"First," Perry said, ignoring this remark, "you two are going to lure Valdez into a trap by letting him follow you here. Only after he's killed will we turn Mankiller loose on Fargo."

Skye Fargo patrolled quietly along the American side of the Rio Grande, keeping the riding thong off the hammer of his Colt.

The moon was in full phase and would remain so for two

more days. That was a twin-edged sword: It made it easier to scout his surroundings after dark, but also made him an easier target.

At the point where the Rio twisted closest to the dry channel behind it, Fargo dismounted and inspected the riverbank for signs of human activity. He found neither human nor horse tracks, only those of smaller animals. So far, at least, it appeared that no blast preparations had been made.

Unless, he reminded himself, some other spot had been picked. But in the case of the first blast, Winslowe's criminals had rerouted the river at its closest point to the secondary channel. Fargo was no engineer, but logic told him that location not only provided a greater chance of success; it would also appear more like an act of nature, not man.

Would the telegram he sent today to Colonel Evans do any good? Trying to second-guess the army was like trying to identify faces in the clouds. Even if Fargo's report was taken seriously, he was certain no action would be taken in time to prevent the second explosion he was convinced was imminent.

Which placed the unwelcome responsibility for stopping it squarely on Fargo's shoulders.

He mounted again and reined the Ovaro around to gauge how close this point was to the long building used by the Phalanx. Less than the distance he could throw a stone, and easily within the blast radius . . .

But again a grin tugged at his lips as he gazed out across the moon-burnished fields. Evidently his "lecture" earlier had taken some effect: Several large fires burned on the far side of the fields, and he could spot human figures moving in and out of the light.

Still others, however, moved about inside the building. It seemed that he had succeeded only in dividing the utopians into two factions, the cautious and the defiant.

The grin quickly melted away, though, when he reminded himself of the daunting reality he faced. An Apache assassin who Valdez assured him was the best on the frontier was likely on his spoor even now. And because Fargo felt obligated to monitor the river closely, he was making the killer's job of finding him easier.

The readiness is all, Fargo reminded himself. And readiness was all he really had.

He rode in a slow circle around the settlement. By now he was familiar with the color and markings of most of the horses in Tierra Seca as well as the mounts of the two mercenaries working for Winslowe. He spotted neither horse at the cantina or at Rosario's house.

Fargo still had a piece of unfinished business. He had done his best to warn the residents of the Phalanx about the potentially devastating blast coming up. But a chunk of Tierra Seca itself, including the busy cantina, was also in harm's way.

Fargo tied off at the snorting post out front and stepped through the archway of the cantina, his eyes darting quickly around the stuffy, smoke-filled interior. The usual lidded, hostile eyes sized him up before sliding away. A few friendlier types recognized him and nodded. A Mexican in a sombrero dozed over his accordion, a victim of too much pulque.

Fargo paused to watch a version of arm wrestling popular in *la frontera*. Two scorpions, their legs tied with thread but stingers intact, had been placed atop a table on both sides of the competing men so that the hand of whoever lost, or was forced too low, would be trapped against the scorpion. One of the men, his strength about to give out, wisely relaxed his arm all at once so the winner drove his hand down hard onto the scorpion, crushing it before it could sting.

Fargo bellied up to the crude plank bar.

"Muy buenas noches, Senor Fargo," Antonio Two Moons greeted him. *"Una copa?"*

Fargo nodded and planked his two bits. Two Moons poured the cactus liquor into a wooden cup. As he placed it in front of Fargo he leaned closer to be heard above the drunken din.

"Senor, I have a—what is the word in your tongue?—a *mensaje* for you."

"A message?"

"Yes. From Santiago Valdez. It is a leetle, how you say, strange."

"He was in here today?"

"Anoche. But this first time I see you. Valdez say to tell you, if you find him dead, look in"—Two Moons lost the words and switched to Spanish—*"en el bolsillo de su camisa."*

120

Fargo's brow wrinkled in puzzlement. "If I find him dead, look in his shirt pocket? Are you sure that's what he said?"

"I think so maybe."

Fargo suspected something had been fractured in the translation. He downed his pulque and said, "Well, I have something to tell you, too."

Keeping his wording simple, Fargo gave Antonio the same warning he had delivered to the Phalanx earlier. Two Moons listened politely as one might do to humor a likable madman.

"Senor Fargo," he said with a shrug when the Trailsman fell silent, "our fate is in the hands of God, not men."

Fargo had expected a reaction of this type. The deeply held fatalism of the Mexican people was not surprising. Theirs was a violent, turbulent, corrupt country where despotic governments were overthrown every few years by the latest "general" capable of raising a drunken army. In these chaotic and lawless conditions men felt no sense of control over their own destiny and left their fate in the hands of God and the beloved saints, the only things—besides suffering—left for them to believe in.

Fargo gave up and left the cantina. Weariness was starting to make his limbs feel heavy and he knew he'd have to soon find a place to bed down. But he decided to take one last look near the river.

This time, to lower his profile against that big, full moon, Fargo led the Ovaro. The Rio purled gently on his left as he walked along the bank, listening carefully.

In the distance a coyote raised its mournful, ululating howl. Only moments after the sound began, Fargo heard a quick scuttling sound behind him. He drew his Colt and thumb-cocked it even as he tucked and rolled, coming up on one knee searching for a target.

He was just in time to spot the distinctive white band of a javelina, small wild hogs found in the deep Southwest and throughout Mexico. It tore off into the night even as the howl of the coyote trailed off in a series of sharp, yipping barks.

"Steady on, Fargo," he warned himself in a whisper. "The worst is yet to come."

16

Once again Fargo rode out into the open desert to catch a few hours of "waking sleep." As he lay under the star-shot sky, grateful for the cool night breeze, he wondered about the strange message from Valdez.

If Two Moons had understood it correctly, it sounded to Fargo like Valdez was anticipating some kind of dangerous confrontation—one he wasn't sure he would survive. Had he finally located the man who raped and killed his wife? Just as puzzling, why did he think Fargo would find his body? Nor could Fargo even guess what might be found in his pocket.

The Ovaro, ground tethered near at hand, was quiet. But the stallion was not infallible, and twice Fargo pushed to his feet and walked, crouching low, in circles around his simple cold camp, Colt in hand. He had picked a barren spot atop a rise, affording him a good view in all directions. Even the most skilled Apache would play hell sneaking up on him here.

Fargo saw nothing but the pale glow of moonlit sand, heard nothing but the wind sighing. But he couldn't forget the old warning about Apaches: *Worry when you see them. Worry more when you don't.*

As Fargo lay with his head against his saddle, half-asleep, half-awake, the fingers of his mind turned his problems over carefully, studying every aspect. So far he had mostly been letting others force his hand—reacting rather than taking charge. Yes, he had gotten the drop on archer Johnny Jackson and he had confronted and surprised Winslowe.

But what had come of his visit to Winslowe? And earlier today, when he took the bull by the horns and attacked Winslowe's hired shit-jobbers—what was the good of it? Even his attempts to warn the residents of Tierra Seca had shown limited success.

Fargo had to face it: So far he was running hard just to stand still. He was up against a criminal cabal with money and privilege at the top and savvy thugs at the bottom as well as a feared assassin perhaps closing in on him right now.

He couldn't attack at the top, Fargo reasoned, without dancing on air or becoming a fugitive. But the bottom was, after all, the foundation, and without the foundation a structure must fall.

The assassin was the greatest threat to his life, but Fargo was forced to face that threat when it came. The thugs, however, were the real key. It was almost certainly they who had executed the first river blast and they who would execute the next one.

Which forced Fargo to an unpleasant but necessary conclusion: Valdez be damned, he must return to Scorpion Town before sunrise and gun both of them down in their room. It might technically be murder, in the myopic eyes of the law, but they had attempted to kill him several times and they would probably kill many innocents if they successfully blasted the Rio Grande again at Tierra Seca.

He had given his word to Valdez, but it was taking too long. The pistolero had a strong personal grudge, and Fargo respected that. But if that blast went forward and Fargo didn't do his utmost to stop it, he would be worse than a man who broke his word.

And if this mysterious Apache succeeded in his mission of killing Fargo, there went the last hope of stopping—or at least delaying—Winslowe's nefarious scheme. Valdez was too wrapped up in his personal vendetta to worry about others, and besides, he might already be dead for all Fargo knew.

The fat is in the fire, Fargo resolved. Earlier he had told the Phalanx he was a majority of one. Now it was time for that majority to act before it was too late.

Early in the morning of his eighth day in the borderland, Skye Fargo roused himself well before sunup.

False dawn glowed pale in the eastern sky. In the open desert, with its clear, transparent air, this glow provided surprising illumination. The Ovaro was quiet as Fargo tacked him, but appeared nervous. The stallion kept arching his neck to stare toward the west, nose constantly sampling the air.

"'S'matter, old campaigner?" Fargo said softly. "You caught a scent?"

Expecting to find nothing, but playing it cautious, Fargo crouched low and began walking west, eyes intently studying the ground.

Fewer than ten feet from where he had lain dozing he suddenly drew up short, his face draining cold.

He had discovered a double line of half-circle depressions that his experienced eye recognized immediately. They had been made by someone wearing soft moccasins and walking on his heels, Indian fashion, to minimize his tracks.

Fargo followed them for perhaps fifty yards until he discovered the likely scent troubling the Ovaro: a fresh pile of horse droppings. Unshod hooves led up to the spot and then away.

The overlapping prints were two-and-a-half to three feet apart, meaning the rider had walked the horse in and away. Sweat formed on Fargo's scalp.

The Apache. And evidently Valdez hadn't exaggerated his skill. It would take an exceptional man to get that close to the Ovaro without alarming the horse.

But if he was an assassin, Fargo asked himself, why didn't he kill me? He was close enough to have done it easily.

Indians, he reminded himself as he returned to his horse, were extremely notional. They didn't think like white men, and their logic was completely different. Perhaps he was toying with his prey—a form of counting coup in which a brave spares his enemy's life, first time around, to let him know he was up against a better man.

Except that Apaches didn't normally count coup or take scalps. They were brutally practical.

Fargo forked leather and gazed all around him in the pale, ghostly light, his confidence shaken. All his precautions had been for naught. He was alive only because of an enemy's whim, and that boded ill for Fargo's future survival.

The Ovaro wanted to run in the cool of early morning and Fargo gave him his head, arriving on the eastern outskirts of

El Paso a full hour before sunrise. He stalled the Ovaro, paying the *mozo* extra for grain and a rubdown, and hoofed it across Paisano Street into Scorpion Town.

It was still too early for most of the denizens of the criminal hellhole to be out and about, and the worst Fargo had to contend with was the foul stench. He relied on his mind map to negotiate the warren of alleys. He noticed, when he arrived at the door of the thugs' rented room, that someone had hauled off the two corpses he'd left last time he was here.

Fargo took his bar key and slid the correct bit into the slot. He glanced behind him to make sure the alley was clear of predators, then stood with his ear to the door for a full two minutes. He heard nothing from within and hoped he had caught the two asleep.

Fargo remembered how loudly the door had creaked open last time, and he didn't bother with finesse. He slid his Colt out and drew the hammer back to full cock. The moment the lock snapped open he flung the door wide and dove inside, coming up on his heels with his short iron aimed toward the crude shakedowns.

There was enough light by now to show him the room was empty. The clothes that had been scattered around like discarded banana peels were gone; there were no blankets on the shuck mattresses; even the pile of tin cans and empty bottles was gone.

Fargo tasted the bitter acid of disappointment. They had moved. Again they were one step ahead of him. Obviously everyone on Stanley Winslowe's payroll played it safe.

But it was still early, Fargo reminded himself. If they were still using the livery stable run by Benito Gonzalez, on the western flank of Scorpion Town, he might be able to spot them when they came for their horses. It was more public, and thus more risky, but Fargo intended to air them out from ambush and be done with it.

He walked back across Paisano Street and searched for a good vantage point. The best spot was that pile of empty hogsheads in front of the warehouse where he had hidden when he watched the livery a few days ago. But he had only been spying then. Today he planned to be shooting, and there was a worker there who kept a close eye on things. That meant a potential witness.

Fargo settled for the recessed doorway of a burned-out harness shop kitty-cornered to the livery. The angle was tricky, but traffic was light and it was an easy range for the Henry. However, two agonizingly slow hours ticked by and neither man showed.

The Trailsman lost patience and crossed the street, entering the hoof-packed yard of the livery. He walked through the open front doors of the barn and waited a moment for his eyes to adjust to the dimness. Then he started to move farther inside.

A menacing click to his left stopped Fargo in his tracks.

"Mister," said a gravelly voice in good, barely accented English, "I been watching you spy on this place for the past couple hours. You ain't got no horse, and you're loaded for bear. The last two cockroaches who tried to steal a horse from here ended up sucking wind."

Fargo glanced in the direction of the voice. A Mexican who looked to be at least sixty, with a sere, weather-grooved face and a hard stare that would back down a charging grizzly, sat on a wagon tongue aiming a hogleg pistol at him.

"I take it you're Benito Gonzalez," Fargo said.

"Names don't mean shit around here. What are you after?"

"Just information, not a horse."

"Then buy yourself some books. I don't give out information."

Fargo remembered Valdez telling him the old hostler was crooked as cat shit.

"All right," Fargo said, "do you sell it?"

"Nope. Half the hombres who board their horses here got their faces on wanted dodgers. Unless you want to know the difference between a burro and a donkey, I got no information to sell."

"What if I leave you out of it?" Fargo persisted. "What if I just walk past the stalls real quick and glance into them?"

"Way I see it, if I let a man fuck me in the ass, I expect a reach-around."

"I'm not looking for anything quite that personal," Fargo said drily. "I just want a quick look at the horses."

"How much is it worth to you?"

"Two dollars."

Gonzalez spat into the dirty straw at his feet. "Ten dollars."

"Four."

Gonzalez wagged the huge-bore pistol. "How 'bout I just take *all* your money?"

"Big mistake," Fargo said.

Quicker than eyesight the Colt appeared in his hand. A shot echoed in the huge barn, and a few horses whickered. Sparks flew and the hogleg jumped out of the old man's hand.

Fargo's face hardened as gray-white smoke curled from the Colt's muzzle. He cocked it again.

"You're lucky, pepper gut. I shot so many holes into the last jasper who tried to rob me that the flies got in and buzzed him to death."

A grin cracked the Mexican's face. "I said *how* 'bout I just take all your money. I didn't demand it."

"I noticed," Fargo said. "That's why you're still alive."

"I like your style. That line about the flies—that's good. All right, two dollars."

Fargo dug two Liberty silver dollars out of his dwindling cash reserve and handed them over. Then he quickly walked the length of the barn checking each stall. As he had feared, Winslow's jobbers had also switched livery stables or acquired new horses.

Unless, he told himself, they've left the region. That meant he'd never settle his personal blood score with them. But that was a welcome tradeoff if it also meant there would be no second blast.

"Any luck?" Gonzalez called to him as Fargo headed back out of the barn.

"No soap, *viejo*."

"Somebody's going to die, uh?"

"Somebody," Fargo agreed. "But I'm damned if I can tell you who."

Fargo felt his stomach pinching with hunger. He had ridden out that morning without eating, and his meals lately had been sparse. He remembered the delicious hot breakfast he'd enjoyed at the Early Bird Café and began to salivate like a starving man at a banquet. He cut over several blocks to Alameda Street.

Fargo ordered a plate of eggs, spiced chorizo and hot biscuits, paid up at the counter, and turned to find a table. The first person he spotted was Deputy Jim West scowling at him over a mug of coffee. Fargo crossed to his table.

"Mind if I sit here?"

"Knock yourself out. I don't mind associating with known criminals."

Fargo maneuvered his long legs under the table and tied into his food.

"Known criminals?" he repeated around a mouthful of egg. "Bit of a stretch, ain't it?"

"Not the way I see it. I could slap the bracelets on you right now, Fargo. That running gun battle you started yesterday within city limits—two witnesses described a tall man in buckskins riding a black-and-white stallion. That's probable cause, chumley."

"You know how unreliable witnesses can be, Deputy. They hear a few gunshots and they get all exfluctuated."

West snorted. "Fargo, I'm stupid enough to think that you're *trying* to work on the right side of the law, at least as you see it. That's why I haven't jugged you . . . yet."

Fargo chewed, swallowed, nodded. " 'Preciate that, Deputy. I truly do."

"Damn it, Fargo, wipe that smirk off your dial! This ain't some wide-open territory where vigilantes can stand in for sworn officers. If you got some knowledge of a crime, report it. Matter fact, vigilantism is a prison offense in Texas."

"I know that. But there's crimes and then there's *crimes*. And I also know that a fish rots from the top."

Winslowe narrowed his eyes, watching Fargo speculatively. "You're talking about Winslowe, right?"

"I am—him and his well-paid bootlicks. The very same man you and your fellow deputies are protecting night and day. Sure, I can go to the sheriff. And he'll slam my ass right into the pokey. You're only taking honest wages from Winslowe, but I'll guarandamntee you there's others above you who've been bought off with dirty money."

"You're saying Sheriff Harney is crooked?"

"Nope. I don't even know the man. But whether he's straight goods or not, are you willing to vouch for the mayor and the councilmen? Is the governor of Texas a scrubbed angel? How 'bout your senators? It's business as usual and you know it. Men like Winslowe don't need to corrupt the underlings—they go right to the big nabobs."

"I won't even vouch for the sheriff," West admitted. "He collects a 'private tax' on every cathouse in town. But look here, Fargo . . . Harney is middling honest in most matters. You're on to some big deal. I can see that. I know that at least three men are trying to kill you, and I know you think Winslowe is behind—"

"You can shit-can the *think* part," Fargo cut him off. "He's the rainmaker, all right."

"All right, so maybe he is—whatever the hell you're talking about. Just because I took good wages from the rich son of a bitch doesn't mean I stand in thick with him. But what's this 'wandering river' malarkey you gave me at the Del Norte? The minute I relayed your message he turned white as plaster."

Fargo kept chewing and said nothing. West slammed his mug down.

"Fargo, I asked you a question. The hell *is* this big crime and why are you mixed in it up to your eyeballs? And why won't you report it?"

Fargo sopped up egg yolk with a biscuit. "West, I did report it, and to a higher authority."

"You telling me this deal is federal?"

Fargo nodded. "As federal as it gets. And I've already explained why I can't risk telling you. It's not that I don't trust you. It's just that you'll have to take it up the chain to the same nabobs who dance on Winslowe's strings."

A word that West had used a few moments ago sank through to Fargo. "What did you mean when you said you *took* wages from Winslowe? Did you quit guarding his room, or did he cashier you?"

West scowled again. "You like to receive but you never give. With me you play button-button-who's-got-the-button.

But I'm just s'pose to spill my guts for the vigilante hero who takes over my job. Stick your dick in your ear, Fargo, and make a jug handle out of it."

"I've told you more than I should. And like you said, Deputy, I'm mainly working the right side of the law. My ass is on the line, and to give you the straight, there's a good chance I'll soon end up cold as a basement floor. I ain't exactly playing at larks here."

West mulled this for at least ten seconds, his face relenting. "Fargo, it looks like Winslowe has pulled up stakes. He checked out of the hotel early this morning. I checked at the Overland depot, and he hired a special coach this morning to take him to Santa Fe. That's where he lives."

Fargo felt a glimmer of hope. The two thugs had deserted their room and livery, Winslowe had left town . . . was it possible he was abandoning his land grab mining scheme, or at least the Tierra Seca part of it?

But if so what about those tracks he found early this morning in the desert, ending only feet from where he'd slept? And Fargo wasn't so full of himself to believe that his brief visit to Winslowe's suite could put ice in the boots of a greedy, grasping, ruthless mining baron.

After all, Winslowe obviously had a capable lackey in whoever the man was that Santiago Valdez was hunting with a desire like hell thirst. Perhaps Winslowe had felt enough heat to remove himself from the area, but Fargo doubted that this fandango was over.

"Well," Fargo said, scraping his chair back, "thanks for the information."

"Hang on a minute," West said. "There's something else."

He studied Fargo for a few moments, seeming to debate something in his mind.

"I don't know why I'm telling you this," he finally said. "You'll prob'ly end up turning another part of town into a war zone. But . . . I noticed that Winslowe had himself a private messenger system. He didn't use the regular runners, and I figure that was on account of the red caps they wear."

"Too easy to spot and follow, you mean?"

West nodded. "There was this fellow, s'pose to be a drummer selling ladies notions, staying on the fourth floor.

But I checked with the desk clerk, and Winslowe was paying for his room—five dollars a night, mind you. Almost every day he came to Winslowe's suite, and left a minute later."

"And I'd wager he checked out this morning just like Winslowe?"

"Yeah. Anyhow, one time the door was partway open and I heard Winslowe mention Mesa Street. That's all I heard. That's the street at the foot of the Franklin Mountains."

Finally, Fargo thought. Just maybe this card would close a straight. But had Valdez already found this out? He hadn't popped up lately as he usually did.

"I 'preciate that information, Deputy."

"Damn it, Fargo, you *listen* to me. Mesa Street is a nice part of town, one of the few. There's families living there. You start chucking lead around there, and women and kids could get hurt. If that happens, I will make sure the law comes down on you like all wrath. You got that?"

"I got it," Fargo said, pushing to his feet. "I'm not planning to start any trouble."

"Jesus! *Start* trouble? Fargo, you *are* trouble. It arrives with you."

Fargo shrugged one shoulder and mustered a grin. "The whole damn world is going insane, Deputy West. I'm just proud to be part of it."

17

West hadn't lied about Mesa Street, Fargo realized.

Fargo had been to El Paso many times, but he hadn't realized such a street as this peaceful, pleasant one existed. Creosote had been spread along the street to hold down the dust, and it had been neatly ditched to catch floodwater during the city's rare but near-torrential downpours.

The street was a six-block stretch lined on both sides with neat cottages and bungalows. A small canyon behind it was lush with blue columbine and white Queen Anne's lace, and beyond it to the northeast pine-forested mountains thrust into a China blue sky. These inhabitants were not wealthy, Fargo figured, just hardworking savers.

He spotted children playing and parcel-laden women returning from their shopping. The residents eyed him with wary curiosity, unused to seeing a buckskin-clad frontiersman in their tame and respectable neighborhood.

Fargo felt like an intruder. No gunplay, he resolved, no matter what. This was no place for stray bullets. But he already had his doubts about what Jim West had overheard. And even if the man Valdez sought had been staying here someplace, was he still here? Valdez had complained about how often he shifted his location. It was also possible that the entire pack of vermin, from bottom to top, had departed El Paso.

Fargo trotted the Ovaro slowly along the street, studying each dwelling. He had already ridden around back of each row of houses to look for horses. He had spotted two, both swayback and neither one young or strong enough to serve as a good mount for outlaws.

Again Fargo felt the familiar frustration that had plagued him since witnessing that blast eight days ago. These men were as elusive as a forgotten dream. Almost every "lead" he followed ended up as a blind alley; every stone he turned over was blank on both sides. He could hardly go knocking on every door, and if he knocked on the wrong one a hail of unfriendly lead might answer.

"Down to bedrock," he muttered, "and showing damn little color."

The Ovaro tossed his head and whinnied as if mocking him.

"If I want your opinion, you spavined nag," Fargo retorted, "I'll beat it out of you."

And where, he wondered yet again, was Valdez? If the Apache had not already sent him across the River Jordan, he was likely following, trying to follow, or searching for the two dirt-workers. Fargo had to decide whether or not he was going to tell him about Mesa Street.

If Valdez managed to kill Winslowe's top man, that might put the kibosh on the entire operation. Or it might not, in which case a potentially valuable witness against Winslowe would be dead. Not that Fargo had any real hope the mining kingpin would ever stand before the bar of justice.

He reached the end of the street, which simply stopped at a sand hill, and reversed his dust. His only chance, he realized, was to find a good hiding place and stake out Mesa Street in hopes he'd spot one of the thugs coming or going. If—

A rifle shot suddenly cracked the stillness and Fargo felt the wind-rip from the slug as it streaked by his right temple. A couple inches to the left and it would have been a perfect head shot.

A woman screamed and Fargo's first priority was to clear out before an innocent got hurt. He thumped the Ovaro with his heels and the stallion bolted forward as if spring-launched. Fargo borrowed a defensive-riding trick from the Cheyenne and slumped down the Ovaro's left side, clinging to the stallion's neck and leaving only his right leg thrown over the saddle to stay on horseback.

But the Trailsman had forgotten an important detail. Because of the extreme desert heat he had been cinching the girth a bit looser to avoid chafing his horse. The sudden shifting of his weight jerked the saddle around to the left like a loose cigar band, throwing his right leg free even as the shifting motion and his awkward angle popped his left foot out of the stirrup.

Suddenly Fargo found himself with both feet bouncing and dragging on the ground as he desperately tried to retain his precarious grip on the stallion's neck. Another shot rang out, a third, both slugs kicking up plumes of dirt only inches from his crow-hopping body. A desperate Fargo realized that if he lost his tentative grip, he would be exposed in the middle of the street—an easy mark for the shooter.

The Ovaro hadn't slowed, nor did Fargo want him to. Getting out of range was his only salvation, and even as he desperately clung to handfuls of mane he ki-yied the Ovaro to even greater speed.

A fourth shot, a fifth, this one penetrating his saddle fender. Pain hammered Fargo's legs as they dragged and bounced, and the straining muscles in his arms and shoulders felt as if they were being stretched on tenterhooks. But somehow he held on as the Ovaro streaked through an oak grove where Mesa Street terminated, suddenly providing Fargo with good cover.

He let go, bouncing and rolling with dizzying speed through lush grass until he finally came to a stop. He sat up slowly, making sure his bones were still intact. His thick buckskins had protected him from abrasions and friction burns. The Ovaro had stopped out ahead and Fargo whistled him back.

Again he had cheated death almost literally by a hair, but this time it was worth it. Now he not only knew that Winslowe's team was still in the borderland, but that Winslowe's point man was indeed somewhere on Mesa Street. Those shots, however, did not come from any of the houses—the trajectory of the bullets put the shooter directly behind him, most likely in the sand hills beyond the opposite end of Mesa Street.

He could hear alarmed neighbors calling to one another, and Fargo recalled Jim West's stern warning: *You start chucking lead around there and women and kids could get hurt. If that happens I will make sure the law comes down on you like all wrath.*

Fargo was sure no one had been hurt, but the law would certainly be summoned. He hadn't chucked any lead, either, but residents would report his presence as the firing broke out, and that was all the law dogs would need to slap him in irons. Fargo centered his saddle, tightened and cinched the girth and hopped his horse, beating a hasty retreat from El Paso.

For more than an hour Ripley Parker paced impatiently in front of the abandoned mine near Zaragoza, Mexico. Occasionally he stopped to stare anxiously toward the north, muttering a string of curses.

Finally, when the broiling sun was straight overhead, he spotted the coal black stallion loping in.

"Where the hell you been?" Parker demanded when Mankiller reined in.

Mankiller swung down and began stripping the saddle from his mount. "Across border," he replied cryptically.

"Didn't I tell you to wait right here until we were ready for you?"

Mankiller said nothing to this, tossing his saddle into the sand and starting to remove the hair bridle.

"What were you doing north of the border? Did you kill anyone?"

Mankiller shook his head. "Watch blue-eyed one sleep."

Parker started. "You mean you found him?"

Mankiller nodded. He moved into the shadows in front of the mine and began methodically squeezing the India rubber balls. He kept his eyes averted from the cloth-covered kachina in Parker's hand. Parker noticed this.

"Didn't I tell you Blood Clot Man wants Valdez killed first?" Parker demanded.

"No kill. Just look."

"Well, since you had already violated orders and got close enough to watch him sleeping, why didn't you go ahead and kill him?"

"Coyote no howl."

Parker's forehead runneled in confusion. "Coyote no—? *What* coyote?"

135

Mankiller sat down with his broad back to one of the wooden supports of the headframe. He continued to squeeze the balls, saying nothing.

Parker swore in frustration. He unwrapped the kachina. "Look," he commanded. "Blood Clot Man *orders* that you look."

Reluctantly, Mankiller shifted his gaze to the carved wooden doll with the evil eyes.

"Blood Clot Man speaks through me," Parker said. "Now tell him about the coyote howl."

"In Taos," Mankiller's oddly labored voice explained, "old *bruja* throw pointing bones. Bones say Mankiller cure blue-eyed one when coyote howl under full moon."

For Mankiller this amounted to a long-winded speech. Parker decided to tread lightly. If he told the Apache that one form of black magic was bullshit, he might conclude that the Witchery Way was, too. In which case Parker would lose his only control over the most dangerous killing machine he knew of—and the mere thought of the potentially disastrous results suddenly tightened his scrotum.

"All right," he said, covering the kachina again. "But it's Blood Clot Man who calls the shots now. Tonight you and me will ride into El Paso after dark. Two men will lead Valdez to a house there and you will kill him. But Valdez has fast guns. You understand? Guns that other men don't have, new guns that fire faster than any others. You *must* come at him from hiding and kill him quickly."

Mankiller nodded. "Mankiller not kill. Cure."

"Yeah, whatever. After you kill—cure—him," Parker added, "then you cure Skye Fargo, the blue-eyed one. He is even more dangerous. You must do your best work with both men, but especially Fargo."

Mankiller's forearm muscles rippled and undulated under his coarse cotton shirt as he worked the hard rubber balls, muscles so huge they threatened to rip through the fabric.

"I cure them both," came the toneless words from a flat slab of face as expressionless as granite.

18

It was late afternoon when Fargo circled Tierra Seca in several slow passes, studying everything from sun-slitted eyes used to spotting danger. He was certain no one had followed him from El Paso, but not at all certain who might be lurking here.

For a moment he recalled those tracks he had discovered early that morning, tracks ending only ten feet from where he lay resting. Even the Ovaro had not alerted at the intrusion.

Be ready, Fargo warned himself. *It's your only chance.*

He rode straight to Rosario's house and dismounted, throwing the reins forward. He stood to one side of the door and knocked. There was no answer. The latchstring was out and Fargo nudged the door open with the muzzle of his Colt.

The place was empty. Fargo didn't step inside, just looked from the dirt threshold. The single, large room was neat and clean, sparsely furnished, with a web bed projecting from a side wall.

Fargo examined the door before he closed it: one inch of solid oak. Next he walked completely around the house, bent low to study the ground.

A clear, pleasant, feminine voice called to him. "Fargo!"

He glanced toward the Rio and saw Rosario Velasquez walking along the American side, coming from somewhere downriver. He walked down to meet her.

"*Buenas tardes*, pretty lady," he greeted her, tipping his hat.

She sent him a sly, pretty smile. "I saw you circling my house. What were you looking for on the ground?"

"Something I did not find but should have."

"Ah? And did you look inside also?"

"Only from the doorway. I didn't go inside."

"You may if you wish. I have no secrets."

"Rosario," Fargo gainsaid, "secrets are *all* you have."

She turned away from him to gaze over the brown, lazy river. When she spoke, it was in a contemplative tone he had never heard her use.

"Fargo, I have seen the Río Bravo flow so fast and hard it washes cattle along with it. And I have seen it dry to a mere—how you say—tickle."

"Trickle," he corrected her.

"Yes. No one knows about what will happen with this river, and no one knows about what will happen with our lives. It is out of our hands *verdad*?"

"Lady," Fargo said gently, "I know what you're up to."

She refused to look at him. "*De veras?* And what am I up to?"

"There's only one window in your house and there are no footprints in the sand anywhere near it. And that door is too solid to hear anything clearly through it. Valdez hasn't been eavesdropping at your house like both of you claim."

"Oh?"

"You're not an outlaw's whore like you claim, either. Sure, you've lately taken one into your bed. But the purpose isn't to get his money, is it?"

"You seem to know so much. You tell me, *guapo*."

"You and Valdez," Fargo continued, "are working together secretly. He's not coming to your house, so you must be meeting him somewhere else. Did you meet him just now?"

"No," she said, "and I swear that is the truth."

"All right. Maybe he didn't show and you're worried. I'm worried about him, too."

"I am listening," she said. "Continue talking."

"Valdez is a *mestizo* and you're Mexican, so you're not his sister. But the woman he married, Estrella Marina—she was Mexican, right? And she was your sister, wasn't she?"

She continued to gaze toward the river still refusing to answer. Gently, Fargo gripped her slim, finely sculpted shoulders and turned her toward him. A crystal dollop zigzagged down her cheek.

"Not *was* my sister," she corrected him. "*Is.* Just because a filthy gringo pig murdered her does not mean she is no longer my sister."

Fargo nodded. "I first began to suspect something when I realized you were telling me things you didn't need to. And all that bragging about how you are a whore—it seemed phony and put on. I didn't believe for one minute that crap about how you liked a loaded gun held to your head."

"I am a *puta* now," she said bitterly. "I let this pig Deuce Ulrick rut on me. Touching his skin was like touching greasy raw bacon. But I learned things from him."

"Deuce Ulrick, huh? Is he the one with the mean mouth and the two-gun rig?"

She nodded. "You killed Johnny Jackson. The other one, the tall, skinny one with the scarred face, is called Slim. He makes the bombs."

"Well, it's obvious you don't know where the man who killed your sister is hiding. But you know his name, don't you—you and Valdez both?"

"Yes. But Santiago begged me not to tell you until he kills him. That has been our problem since you arrived in *la frontera*—how much we could tell you. Santiago knew your help could be val- val—"

"Valuable?"

"Yes, that. But he also feared you might kill this man before he could."

"When's the last time you talked to Valdez?"

"We rarely talk," she said. "It is too dangerous for both of us. If the gringo pigs ever found out . . . so we leave messages for each other in a, how you say, hollow log by the river. But there has been nothing for days now."

"Yeah, I haven't seen him lately, either. That's why I'm worried. Usually he pops up everywhere I am. He might be dead—the Apache killer is here."

Her eyes widened. "You have seen him?"

Fargo's lips pressed together grimly. "No, but he's seen me. What about Ulrick—does he still come to your house?"

She shook her head. "They both stay away from Tierra Seca now. They have much fear of you."

"They sure don't *act* too afraid. Those two have put me through the grinder. They're not run-of-the-mill criminals."

Fargo was quiet for perhaps fifteen seconds. Then:

"Rosario, I'm pretty sure I've located the man who killed your sister. That is, I'm pretty sure I know what street he's on, and it's a short street."

A transformation came over her beautiful face. The pensive sadness suddenly disappeared, replaced by an urgent need Fargo had seen before—the potent, all-consuming need for blood vengeance.

"Where? Where is the pig?"

"Just hold your powder," Fargo said. "You do know what Stanley Winslowe is doing with the river, right?"

She nodded impatiently. "*What* street?" she demanded.

The fervid, homicidal glint in her eyes warned Fargo against telling her. Many Mexican women were dangerous hotheads in matters of family honor, and she might be foolish enough to try settling scores herself.

"Rosario, do you understand how serious this deal with the river is? And do you know that Tierra Seca could be blown up at any time?"

"*Ya lo veo.* Now I see how it is. You will lose your gringa whores and the cornfield where you take them on the ground like animals!"

Fargo grinned. "Well, there's that. But that's not my point. Don't you care that many people could die?"

"Of course. But is this not one more reason why the pig should be killed *muy pronto*?"

"Maybe yes and maybe no. If he is killed that *might* stop the Tierra Seca blast, but I've met Winslowe, and I wouldn't count on it. And even if he did back off, he's already grabbed a rich chunk of Mexico. That could lead to another U.S.-Mexico war or at least to a bloodbath in the borderland. Maybe if the man who killed your sister can be arrested instead for this land grab there's a slim chance Winslowe, too, might be prosecuted."

"And perhaps the devil will have a fiesta for all the souls in hell! Fargo, you among all men know that law is not *justicia*. It is a whore for the rich and powerful criminals. This Winslowe, nothing will ever stop him and the pigs like him. But if Santiago kills the one who raped and murdered my sister, then it is not only revenge for me and Santiago—you may stop a second bomb and save your gringas and the cornfield where you enjoy them."

Fargo chuckled. "That's twice you've mentioned that cornfield. It seems to be on your mind a lot. Anyhow, the part you said about the law as a whore for the rich makes plenty of sense. And to tell you the truth I've come to the same conclusion. But we don't even know where Santiago is. He might even be dead."

"Then *you* kill this man, Fargo. Santiago told me you can do it. *Please* kill him for my sister and for all the lives you may yet save! This man could flee at any moment."

Fargo wasn't in the business of satisfying the revenge needs of others despite his sympathy for Rosario and her brother-in-law. However, his thinking meshed with hers on the rest of it, especially the very real danger that Winslowe's point man could disappear again at any time.

"I'm going back to El Paso after sundown," he told her. "But all I can do is watch the street and wait. With luck one of these two men, or perhaps Ripley Parker, will show up at the right house."

Her eyes lit up. "I knew you would! You—"

Fargo raised a hand to silence her. "Don't get ahead of the game, Rosario. I also have to assume the Apache could be in the mix. If Santiago is still alive, I'd prefer to have him siding me against so many expert killers."

"Siding? What does this word mean?"

"Helping me," Fargo explained. "He's a famous pistolero."

"Yes. I will put a message in the log. There is not much time but perhaps he would find it. Where would I tell him to meet you?"

Fargo had to be careful here judging from the blazing intensity of Rosario's eyes.

"Tell him I might be waiting in an oak grove at the eastern end of Mesa Street. That's not the street I'm watching," he lied, "but Winslowe's men would have to pass this grove to get to the right street and house."

"Fargo, as you say, Santiago may already be dead. Or he may not come. Do you believe you alone can defeat these men?"

"Anything is possible," he replied. "I've beat long odds before. But to be honest, *chica*, I'm not sure what I'm going to do. I'll place my bet after I see my cards."

A big full moon seemed to be balanced on Ranger Peak, the highest point in the Franklin Mountains just north of El Paso. Fargo approached the end of Mesa Street along a rutted lane that cut through a big sandlot dotted with tufts of wiry palomilla grass.

He was still at least a quarter mile south of the oak grove when he heard it: six muted but rapid gunshots. They sounded exactly like the warning shots Santiago Valdez had fired behind him in the alley yesterday morning to thwart his pursuit of Deuce Ulrick and the rake handle named Slim.

Fargo thumped the Ovaro to a gallop. Just before he reached Mesa Street, he heard two riders pounding past him about thirty yards to his left. Despite the generous moonlight he could not make out their features except that one cut a huge silhouette against the blue-black sky and rode a dark horse with no visible markings.

The moment Fargo thundered onto Mesa Street he spotted a knot of shadowy figures gathered in front of a dwelling about halfway down the left side of the street. Fargo reined to a stop in the street and dismounted, tossing the reins forward. He recognized Ulrick and Slim's mounts hobbled beside the house and Santiago Valdez's roan one block farther down on the opposite side of the street.

Fargo shucked out his Colt and the curious, frightened neighbors parted before him as he approached the cottage. The front door stood halfway open, sending a yellow shaft of lamplight slanting into the small front yard.

The Trailsman eased cautiously through the door and immediately whiffed the acrid stench of spent powder and the sheared-copper odor of fresh blood—lots of blood.

He cleared the short entry hall and glanced to his right, his jaw slacking open in astonishment. Four dead bodies littered the small parlor along with shards of glass from a broken side window. Ulrick and Slim both lay sprawled on their backs, two neat holes in each man's forehead. Blood and brain matter dripped from the wallpaper behind them.

A third man Fargo didn't recognize, a professorial type with gold-rimmed spectacles and a neat spade beard, had fallen backward across a low table. He also sported a pair of neat holes in his forehead. Fargo had no doubt that he was Winslowe's point man and the despicable coward who had raped and killed Valdez's wife.

But it was the sight of the fourth, barely recognizable dead man that made Fargo forget to breathe.

Santiago Valdez lay in a heap in the middle of the room. His face was grotesquely swollen and black, his neck broken—no, not just broken. Valdez's head had literally been twisted around so violently that his dead, glazed eyes were staring straight back over his right shoulder at Fargo.

And there was a huge, bloody cavity in his chest where the heart had been savagely cut out. Since it wasn't lying around in sight, Fargo figured it had been taken.

The Apache's handiwork, a stunned Fargo told himself. And those two riders who fled past him just now were almost certainly the assassin and his handler, Ripley Parker. Fargo knew damn well who was next on their short list.

He also figured that by now someone had gone to fetch the law. But he had to satisfy his curiosity on one point. He quickly checked the thugs' weapons and verified that none had been fired. One of Mean Mouth's Army Colts was missing, and Fargo guessed Parker had grabbed it to replace the horse pistol Fargo had ruined.

One of Valdez's Adams of London experimental double-action repeaters lay a few feet from his body. Fargo checked it and noted that all six chambers were empty.

The second gun was still clutched in his left hand. Fargo pried it loose and immediately noticed a cartridge wedged crookedly between the hammer and the chamber-rotating pawl—the gun had jammed without ever firing.

Valdez's instincts, Fargo realized, had been right all along. He had told Fargo the model was unreliable, but that both guns never jammed at once. And the double-action gun that did fire gave him just enough rapid shots to fulfill the overriding mission of his life: avenging the murder of his beloved wife.

"Good work, Santiago," he muttered. "Damn good work, old son."

Fargo was hustling toward the door when he remembered that message Valdez had sent him through Antonio Two Moons. He turned back, knelt beside Valdez's corpse again, and slipped three fingers into his shirt pocket, extracting a folded sheet of paper.

Fargo tucked it into his possibles bag without looking at it, intent now on only one thing: clearing out before El Paso lawmen made him the scapegoat for all these killings.

19

Fargo rode past the copper mines dotting the eastern edge of El Paso and followed the meanders of the Rio Grande into the desert for several miles, camping in the midst of a mesquite thicket on the American side of the river.

He dug a seep hole in the sand a few feet back from the muddy river, drinking his fill of the cleaner water that filled it. After watering the Ovaro he put the stallion on a long tether so he could graze the tasty mesquite pods.

After seeing what the Apache had done to Valdez, Fargo was filled with a calm, lethal determination to bring this thing to a head. With Winslowe's point man now deader than a Paiute grave, the Trailsman had no idea if he was still a target for assassination. Given his recent thrashing of Ripley Parker, however, Fargo felt it was wise to assume he was.

He had also decided to give Parker and his blue-ribbon killer every opportunity to make their move although it seemed highly unlikely it would come tonight. They had been racing due south at a two-twenty clip when they passed Fargo earlier, probably headed straight into Old Mexico, and he doubted that even the talented Apache could track him to this new camp so soon.

However, Fargo had a new burr under his blanket: El Paso's tough-as-boar-bristles law officers. True, there was no evidence he had been present for any of the killings. And if they had the brains God gave a pissant they could reconstruct events at the crime scene just as Fargo had done.

But the Texas constabulary was notorious for making arrests to save face, and the residents on Mesa Street had seen the buckskin-clad intruder in their neighborhood twice.

In the Lone Star State a man held "on suspicion" could rot in the calaboose for months, even years.

"Pile on the agony," Fargo said out loud.

The Ovaro showed his concern by suddenly sending a load of horse apples loudly plopping to the ground.

"There's a glue factory in your future," Fargo promised.

He built a cooking fire from mesquite wood and boiled a handful of coffee beans before frying up some bacon, eating it out of the hot pan. Afterward, as he drifted down into his first sound sleep in days, an image plagued him: Santiago's glass-marble eyes staring at him from a head twisted half-way around like that of a child's broken doll.

Fargo kicked his blanket off at sunrise and stood up, twisting out the night kinks. He tacked the Ovaro and broke camp. He had just grabbed the saddle horn and was about to hit leather when he stopped himself. Curiosity impelled him to take a quick look at the sandy ground surrounding the thicket.

He had taken only a few steps out into the open when Fargo felt his blood turn to icy slush.

"Son of a *bitch*," he said out loud, dumbfounded.

How? And *why*?

The half-circle prints were back again, stopping only about ten feet from where he had lain sleeping. How could the Apache possibly have found him so quickly, how did he again slip up on the ever-vigilant Ovaro, and *why*, Fargo demanded of the cosmos in general, didn't he close for the kill? He certainly hadn't hesitated with Valdez.

There was only one possible explanation for the "how" part of it, Fargo decided. The Apache had recognized him or his horse last night riding toward Mesa Street and waited around, following him to this spot. As to why he hadn't killed him . . . Fargo recalled Valdez explaining that the Apache was an avid believer in Indian black magic. Fargo couldn't figure the angle, but maybe that somehow tied into it.

Still unnerved, Fargo swung up and over and reined the Ovaro back toward El Paso. He knew it was risky as all hell to return after the carnage on Mesa Street last night, but Fargo had told Colonel Evans he would check for any return messages from Fort Union.

He didn't expect anything more than a curt, perfunctory reply if even that. But as Fargo read the yellow flimsy the clerk handed out the window, his opinion of Colonel Josiah Evans went up a few notches:

HAVE ATTACHED ALL PRIORITY TO YOURS OF 7 SEPTEMBER AND AM ACTING ON MY OWN AUTHORITY. SITUATION POTENTIALLY SERIOUS. ARRIVING ASAP WITH ENGINEERS, DEMO TEAM. YOUR HELP NEEDED TO IDENTIFY SPECIFIC LOCATIONS AND COMPLETE REPORT. CHECK FOR ME AT BALDERAS INN ON TEXAS STREET. YOU ARE ON SALARY AND PER DIEM.

"Did Santiago suffer?" Rosario asked.

"Some," Fargo admitted. "But not nearly so long as his wife must have."

"He was shot?"

"Strangled," Fargo replied, leaving it there. He saw no reason to tell this woman that "strangled" was painting the lily or that her brother-in-law's heart had been cut out and stolen.

It was late morning on Fargo's ninth day in the borderland, and the two of them sat at a table in Antonio Two Moons's cantina. Business was slow and they spoke in low tones, Fargo's eyes constantly darting to the doorway.

"Do you know," she told Fargo, "Santiago always believed he would die avenging my sister? But he also believed he would someday kill Harlan Perry. That is why he bought these strange new guns that you say ja—ja—"

"Jammed," Fargo supplied. "But only one did. So Harlan Perry was the name of the man you both wanted so bad?"

Rosario nodded, her pretty face sad at the news of Valdez. "It is an odd thing, Fargo. For so long Santiago and I planned for the death of Perry. Now it has finally come to pass and I feel little joy. Only a great relief that it is finally done."

"Revenge," Fargo replied, "isn't always sweet, especially since it cost Santiago his life. But he would have had it no other way."

"*Como no.* He told me once that without Estrella he would have taken his own life. He stayed alive only to kill Perry. Perhaps, after all, it was best that he died. Fargo, how can one man be like you and another like Santiago?"

147

Fargo raised a puzzled eyebrow. "You wanna chew that a little finer?"

"About women, I mean. Santiago was a handsome man like you, and women were drawn to him. But in all this world he loved only one woman. No other even tempted him. But you . . . you are like a bee sampling flowers, and you never return to the same flower twice."

"Now, that's a slander on me," Fargo protested. "Twice is generally my minimum—sometimes I return to the same flower four or five times in less than an hour."

She slapped his arm playfully. "Again you boast to get me excited. I confess I am more like you than like Santiago—I, too, like to sample different flowers. But perhaps you will not wish to touch me after I was with—"

"Lady," Fargo interrupted her, "I been thinking about 'touching' you ever since I first laid eyes on you. But it's a bad idea right now. That hell-spawned Apache who killed Santiago is after me now, and I'd best keep my wits about me or he'll be using my teeth for dice. Matter fact, me and you are not going to see each other again until I've settled up with him—one way or the other."

"But why would he kill you now? Perry hired him, and he is dead."

"Actually, it's Stanley Winslowe who pays the bills. Besides, Ripley Parker controls the Apache, and Parker wants my guts for tipi ropes."

Fargo pulled a folded paper from his possibles bag and began to unfold it on the table.

"What is that?" Rosario asked.

"A map that Santiago drew," Fargo replied. "I glanced at it last night. I had words with him one time about the fact that he didn't give a damn about anything except killing Perry. But this map shows where Winslowe's vermin buried their explosives. Santiago wanted to help after all, but he figured he had to wait until he killed Perry or died trying."

"Yes, but that does not matter now, *verdad*? Ulrick and the skinny bomb maker are dead."

"Parker isn't. Depending on how close he worked with the others, he might know where the stuff is. And guncotton—that's the explosive—is easy to use. He wouldn't likely know exactly how to plant it to shape the charge, but that might not stop him from trying. There's a reasonable chance he at least knows the spot where they planned to blast the river, and if so, he could do a lot of damage here in Tierra Seca."

Rosario backhanded a renegade strand of hair from her eyes. "I was like Santiago—only killing Perry mattered. Now he is dead and I feel shame. Many here could die. But you said soldiers are coming?"

"Yeah, but they'll take at least three or four days. I have to blow this stuff up on the off chance Parker means to carry out the plan before then."

Rosario thought of something. "If Parker knows where it is, he can show the Apache also, *verdad*? And they may guess you will try to destroy it and wait for you there."

" 'Fraid so," Fargo said. "But I don't think that Apache needs to be told a damn thing or wait in one spot for me. I'm wondering if he's even human."

"You can defeat him," Rosario said confidently. "You are the Trailsman."

"Whipping him is the plan, all right. But I've had bad luck ever since I got here. Winslowe's thugs were always just a little bit too smart for me."

"Santiago said it was you who were too smart for them."

"I only managed to notch my sights on one of them. It was Santiago who killed the other two. And twice now that damn Apache has sneaked close enough to spit on me. I need better cards or a fresh deck."

"*Vaya!* Is the army not sending men down here because of your report? Santiago told me how Winslowe's *criminales* tried many times to kill you, and each time you sent them running. He told me you saved his life during their first attack. And he said they became so—how you say—afraid of you that *finalmente* they stayed away from you and only watched you."

"I s'pose all that's so. But it's not just about staying alive and scaring men off. When they're trying to kill you, you have to kill them first. This Apache isn't afraid of any man, and once he decides to close for the kill, I better be one second faster."

Rosario suddenly looked troubled. "Fargo, you speak of this Apache killer. Do you believe in the power of dreams?"

"Not so's you'd notice. Why do you ask?"

"Last night . . . I did not yet know that Santiago was dead. Yet, his ghost appeared to me in a dream. His"—she crossed herself before going on—"his chest was ripped open and, Blessed Virgin, his heart was gone."

Fargo felt the hair on his nape stand up. He hadn't said a word about that to Rosario.

"He said only one thing to me," she pressed on. "He told me: 'Tell Fargo the Apache is coming for him, and the only way he can survive is to die before he is dead.' In the dream I asked him what this meant, but he faded away without answering."

"Die before I'm dead?" Fargo repeated.

She nodded. "What can it mean?"

"Damned if I know," Fargo replied, "but I hope I figure it out quick."

20

Ripley Parker was stewing in his own juices.

Yes, Mankiller had succeeded in killing Valdez last night. But everything had gone to hell from the moment the half-breed son of a bitch had surprised everyone by diving through a side window instead of using the unlocked front door behind which Mankiller was waiting.

Parker still couldn't believe it. Valdez had tumbled into the room, come up onto his heels with gun blazing, and—never needing to cock his hammer even once—cut down Perry, Deuce Ulrick and Slim Robek in about three seconds flat. If that second gun of his hadn't jammed, Parker knew that he and Mankiller, too, would be walking with their ancestors.

But that wasn't the half of it. Mankiller had picked up Skye Fargo's trail last night and successfully tracked him to his camp beside the Rio Grande. And for the second night in a row the big, dumb, superstitious bastard had passed up a golden opportunity for an easy kill because "coyote no howl."

Parker knew how to contact Stanley Winslowe in Santa Fe, but money and further orders weren't the issue now. Fargo was an implacable force and had to be killed. Parker allowed no man to beat him down as Fargo had thrashed him, and only Mankiller could settle that score. And yet . . . just *look* at the disgusting son of a bitch!

His stomach churning, he watched the Apache run a spit through Valdez's heart and hold it over a fire to roast.

"Mankiller," he growled, anger spiking his voice and echoing in the abandoned mine, "you *can't* keep letting Fargo off the hook. Forget about this shit with a coyote howling. That old crone up in Taos just made that up."

Mankiller said nothing to this, turning the heart to scorch the outside evenly. He believed Maria Santos's prophesy, but he was worried. Tonight was the last night the moon would be in full phase until three more weeks passed. But still the coyote had not howled. Why?

Perhaps an enemy's bad medicine was interfering?

"*Listen* to me, damn you!" Parker exploded. "You know that I speak for Blood Clot Man. He says to never mind about a coyote howling and just kill Fargo, the blue-eyed one."

Still Mankiller held silent. By now the heart was scorched on the outside. He bit into the hot, tasty meat and solemnly began chewing.

Parker avoided retching only by a supreme effort. He jumped to his feet and pulled the cloth away from the evil kachina doll.

"*Look* at Blood Clot Man!" he commanded.

Reluctantly Mankiller did, pausing in his chewing. The doll's dark, evil eyes seemed alive to him, emanating straight from the Forest of Tears—the red man's equivalent of white man's hell.

But this time they seemed to be talking to him, trying to convey an important message.

"*Don't* fuck with Blood Clot Man!" Parker snarled. "He can turn you into worm shit if you disobey him. Damn it, man, kill Fargo next chance you get! I'll be hog-tied and earmarked before I let that crusading bastard get away with thumping on me like he—"

Parker suddenly caught himself, realizing his mistake. A genuine *brujo* would not be subject to beatings from any man.

"Like he *wants* to do," he lamely amended.

Mankiller had seen the tape around Parker's ribs as well as the obvious broken nose and teeth. He set the partially eaten heart aside and shifted his atavistic eyes from the kachina to Parker. "You say fall from horse."

"I did. I'm saying Fargo would *like* to beat on me. Of course he can't because I live by night just like Blood Clot Man and my medicine is too strong."

Parker's voice sounded nervous, wheedling. Mankiller shifted his gaze back to the eyes of the kachina. Again it seemed like they were talking to him.

"The coyote has not howled," he suddenly addressed himself directly to the carved wooden doll for the first time. "Tell me why."

Parker looked confused. "Who the hell are you talking to?"

But Mankiller did not answer him because now the kachina was speaking clearly in the Apache's mind.

The coyote has not howled, Blood Clot Man told him, because you follow a false *brujo*. I do not speak through this weak white dog. Your mother was a powerful *bruja* and mistress of the Witchery Way. Her power flows in you, not in this cowardly whiteskin.

Mankiller pushed to his feet.

"The hell you doing?" Parker demanded, his voice now reedy with fright.

Mankiller started toward him. Parker backed away, thrusting the kachina out before him. "Blood Clot Man will pray you into the ground if you don't obey him!"

He does not cure the disease of life, Blood Clot Man said in Mankiller's mind. The white dog only uses you to kill the man who defeated him.

Still Mankiller advanced. Parker, in a welter of fright, threw the doll down and clawed for the Army Colt in his belt, the weapon he had taken from Deuce Ulrick's corpse last night.

But Mankiller was surprisingly fast for such a big man. He closed the gap in a heartbeat. He gripped Parker's arm at the forearm and elbow and flexed his muscles, snapping the bone like a dry stick. Jagged edges of broken white bone tore through the skin, and Parker howled in pain as he dropped the weapon.

He abruptly ran out of retreating room, his back bumping against the side of the mine tunnel. The big hands, each finger like a thick rope, rose toward his throat.

"No!" he screamed in a voice gone raspy with terror.

Yes, Blood Clot Man urged inside the mind of the Apache. *Cure him so the coyote will howl!*

At first, following Valdez's quickly sketched map had proved easy. A dotted line led from Tierra Seca east to a wide bend in the river. A second line led due north for about a hundred yards to a circle labeled "black rocks." Fargo found it quickly, a small heap of cinder rocks from some long ago era when molten lava had poured over the region.

Valdez had marked the river bend and rocks to give Fargo fixed references in the desolate landscape. But things got harder after that. Another dotted line led north-northeast from the rocks an indeterminate distance to a dot labeled simply "knoll." However, several knolls in the area could have been the one indicated by the inaccurate map.

"He was a good pistolero," Fargo remarked to himself as he gazed at the confusing terrain. "But he was poor shakes as a topographer."

Fargo began by examining each knoll for prints or signs of digging. But this section of the borderland was loose, shifting sand pummeled by stiff winds that would have quickly erased any clues. Under a punishing afternoon sun that had weight as well as heat, he used his small entrenching tool and began the search for the buried explosives.

Fargo had learned by now not to underrate the Apache assassin who most likely was still dogging him. As he worked, moving from knoll to knoll, he watched in every direction. Shimmering heat waves danced over the desert sand and forced him to even more careful scrutiny.

Tell Fargo he must die before he is dead.

Rosario's strange dream kept running through Fargo's thoughts. He had never set any store in spirit knockings, crystal balls, séances and the other "third eye" foolishness that captivated so many in America. But Rosario could not possibly have known about the gruesome fact that Valdez's heart had been cut out, and yet, it was in her dream.

But *how* could a man die before he was dead?

After two hours of useless digging Fargo debated the idea of giving up. After all, there was a good chance that Ripley Parker and the Apache knew nothing about the location of the buried explosives. But what if Parker did know and decided to use them? Fargo had spent the last nine days putting his ass on the line, and he couldn't bring himself to roll the dice now with the fate of Tierra Seca in the balance.

Another hour passed and Fargo had been laboring under the cruel sun so long that black dots were dancing in front of his eyes. He was about to give it up as a bad job when the tip of his entrenching tool struck something solid.

Five minutes later, with the sun now rapidly descending, it was all spread out in the sand before him: a canvas ground-sheet upon which sat eight blocks of guncotton that had been steeped in nitric and sulfuric acids, and a can of the primer known as cotton powder.

Working quickly before the sun set, Fargo stacked the blocks of guncotton back in the hole to concentrate them. He dug a small trench and lined it with the cotton powder primer as a fuse. The Rio Grande wound its way about a quarter mile due south of him, and the moment Fargo flipped a burning lucifer into the fuse trench he vaulted onto the Ovaro and raced toward the river even as the bloodred sun flamed out in the west.

He was perhaps halfway to the river when a massive boom-crack behind him stung his eardrums and sent a concussive wave slamming harmlessly into horse and rider. Falling sand pelted them and Fargo fought to settle the spooked stallion.

Fargo was hot, parched with thirst and sticky from the salty residue of so much evaporated sweat coating him like grease. He headed for a clump of cottonwoods beside the river and reined in, hobbling his still-nervous mount.

The spot seemed safe. Birds chattered, cicadas gave off their monotonous drone, and the lazy Rio Grande chuckled softly. A full moon glowed, spider-webbed by the tree branches overhead. Fargo took a careful look around and then began digging a seep hole a few feet back from the river.

He paused often to watch and listen. Fargo had learned that impending danger often lent a certain texture to the air, and suddenly he felt it now: a galvanic tickle of charged air parti-cles as if a huge bolt of lightning were about to fork down from the heavens.

He knocked the riding thong off the hammer of his Colt and loosened the weapon in its holster, every sense acutely alert. If it was coming, let it come.

He suddenly started when a nearby coyote began its long, mournful howl. In the same moment a dark, massive figure lunged from behind a nearby cottonwood and Fargo's right hand streaked toward his holster.

21

The lightning-swift attacker beat Fargo's gun hand by a fractional second.

The air was thumped from his chest when the huge assailant bowled into him, knocking the Colt from his hand. It was all too quick to comprehend. Fargo was driven backward by the attacker's weight and felt a sudden, jarring slam against his back as he crashed hard into the ground.

The double impact, front and back, was like being caught in the cross kick of two powerful mules. Fargo saw a bright orange pinwheel explode inside his skull. But by sheer dint of will to survive he fought off the dark oblivion of unconsciousness, teetering on the brink of awareness.

He felt two huge, powerful hands encircle his neck.

Fargo had been choked before, but this was terrifyingly different. The flow of blood and air were both stopped immediately, and the viselike power of the grip defied belief. He saw the Apache's stone-carved face in the moonlight, those dead black-button eyes never once blinking as they bored into him. Still throttling him the Apache rose and effortlessly picked him up off the ground.

Fargo, badly stunned, could not muster the strength to fight this bear, though every instinct in his body urged him to struggle even without breath. So he did although his efforts were useless. Death was coming for him on incredibly swift wings; his world was closing down to darkness and raw pain.

Tell Fargo he must die before he is dead.

And then Fargo understood.

There were still a few more heartbeats of struggle and awareness left in him. But instead he pretended to die. He suddenly slumped heavily and went slack, perfectly feigning death while actually on the threshold.

Mankiller was disappointed, even in his elation. He had expected more of a fight from this formidable-appearing, blue-eyed frontiersman. Instead, he turned out to be nearly as fragile as a woman. His heart was not worth eating.

Mankiller threw the dead man down in disgust. And Old Maria had called him "a worthy foe."

A few eyeblinks later, cold, hard steel slid between his fourth and fifth ribs and pierced deep into his heart as the supposedly dead Fargo rose to his knees and drove the Arkansas toothpick hard with his last reserve of strength. The Apache sucked in a final breath, staggered, collapsed onto the ground.

Fargo lay still for several minutes gasping for air. When he finally sat up and gingerly touched his neck, shock jolted through him. His neck was so swollen that he could barely differentiate it from his chin.

He glanced at the dead Apache in the eerie, blue-white moonlight. He was sprawled on his back and something protruded from the folds of his shirt. Fargo pulled it out and recognized the carved kachina doll, its evil face now glistening with the Apache's blood.

"Thanks for the warning, Santiago," Fargo muttered hoarsely. "I died before I was dead and now I'm alive."

"Good God, Fargo!" fumed Colonel Josiah Evans. "I said you were on per diem, not a drunken spree!"

He stared in disbelief at the bill a desk clerk at the Balderas Inn had just handed him. "Sixteen dollars for your room, eight dollars for meals . . . a liquor tab for *twelve* dollars! Are you trying to bankrupt the U.S. Treasury?"

"I earned it," Fargo assured him. "Besides, this river deal cost me a lot of my own money. I had to pay for—"

Evans raised a hand to silence him. "Spare me the sob story. I'll authorize payment. It pains me to say it, but you certainly did earn it. You may be an irreverent reprobate, but I must admit that you have rendered a great service to your nation."

The two men sat, smoking Evans's cigars, on a sofa in the small but comfortable lobby. As Fargo had predicted, it had taken U.S. Army engineers less than one hour to confirm Fargo's report: The Rio Grande had indeed been blasted out of its natural channel and routed into an older one. A strategically placed countercharge had returned to Mexico the silver-bearing ridges stolen by Stanley Winslowe.

Fargo let the colonel's remark pass without comment. But the Trailsman's concept of "nation" was vastly different from the colonel's. For Fargo it was the land itself, the mountains and deserts and rivers and plains, the wide-open spaces and remote canyons—the pristine frontier that greedy money grubbers like Winslowe treated as their personal cash cows. If Fargo had saved innocent life during his recent ordeal, all well and good. But thwarting a wealthy criminal like Winslowe was the real prize.

"Tell me the truth, Colonel," Fargo said. "Is there even a snowball's chance Winslowe will face a trial?"

Evans expelled a long, frustrated sigh. "Don't hold your breath. I'll file a report, of course. But I failed completely, a couple years back, to get an indictment against his man Harlan Perry for attempted bribery. United States attorneys are handmaidens to the politicos, and if I can't hobble the sub-chief, I'll certainly not hobble the chief."

"Well," Fargo said, tossing back his head and blowing a perfect smoke ring, "at least you won't have to worry about Perry anymore."

Evans sent him a sharp glance. "Yes, I read all about that in the local newspaper. Some local legend named Santiago Valdez and a vengeance killing . . . evidently the man has become quite a folk hero since that bloody incident, even on this side of the border. And I noticed your name was linked to his, although vaguely."

"Oh, you might say we were nodding acquaintances," Fargo said dismissively.

"I'm sure you were," Evans said sarcastically. "According to the newspaper accounts, El Paso lawmen suspect it was more than nodding."

"Yeah, they looked me up and did some blustering. But none of the bullets in those dead bodies matched the caliber of my weapons and they lost interest."

Evans said, "There were no bullets in Valdez. Those sensational descriptions of his dead body—were they true?"

"Every word," Fargo admitted.

"So you *were* mixed up in that fray. I wondered about those marks on your neck. But who on God's green earth could have done that to him?"

"He's no longer on God's green earth," Fargo replied. "Unless you count skeletons. Desert buzzards work fast."

Evans frowned. "I see that, as usual, you've left plenty out of your report."

"Nothing that mattered to the army," Fargo assured him.

"Well, I must admit that your penchant for, ah, discretion in one point is commendable: Not one newspaper mentioned the situation with the Rio Grande."

"That's prob'ly luck more than discretion. I did have to tell some people about it."

"At any rate, getting back to Winslowe: While he will likely buy his way out of any legal repercussions, we *have* put the kibosh on his ambitions for stealing Mexican territory. I'm putting him on notice that a report is being filed with the War Department and that the U.S. Army will be monitoring his activities closely. He has too much to lose if he tries another international land grab. Even a rich man can go once too often to the well."

"His ilk always prospers somehow," Fargo remarked. "If they can't raise the bridge, they just lower the river—so to speak."

"No question about it. But, Fargo, I was a young lieutenant of artillery in the Mexican War. I witnessed firsthand the slaughter in battles like Cerro Gordo and Chapultepec. Mexican resentment naturally runs high, and I believe your persistence in exposing Winslowe's actions may well have headed off another vicious conflict. You'll never be a model citizen or even a true-blue patriot, and we have our differences, but you can always count on me for future contract work."

"I 'preciate that, Colonel. I'm generally light in the pockets."

"As a matter of fact," Evans added, "I could use a good chief of scouts for an expedition Headquarters is getting up—an extended patrol across the Continental Divide into

Jicarilla Apache country. I and my team are leaving El Paso today and returning to the fort. Why don't you ride back with us?"

"Sounds good," Fargo agreed, suddenly entertaining a vision of a copper-skinned Mexican beauty with a beguiling smile. "But I'll catch up with you on the trail. I have a little . . . matter to take care of in Tierra Seca."

Evans, who was well known among his soldiers as a prude, shook his head in resigned disapproval. "You and your infernal womanizing. You won't die in the saddle, Fargo—you'll be shot in some married woman's bed."

Fargo didn't see that as such a bad fate, but he assumed the face of an innocent cherub. "You got it all wrong, sir. I'm just riding down to Tierra Seca to sample a flower."

LOOKING FORWARD!
The following is the opening section of the next novel in the exciting Trailsman series from Signet:

TRAILSMAN #389
OUTLAW TRACKDOWN

Wyoming, 1861—where a young killer has gone on a spree and has Fargo in his gun sights.

It isn't every day a man starts a brawl.

Skye Fargo had no intention of starting one when he stopped at the saloon in a sleepy little town called Horse Creek. He had a full poke after being paid for a scouting hitch with the army and figured to treat himself to a bottle of Monongahela, a card game, and a willing dove, not necessarily in that order.

So when he ambled into a whiskey mill called the Tumbleweed, he wasn't looking for trouble. He was looking for a good time.

Fargo strode to the bar and smacked it for service. Not that he need have bothered. Other than an old-timer sucking down bug juice like it was the elixir of life, the only other patrons were three townsmen playing cards.

The bartender waddled over and asked, "What'll it be, mister?"

Fargo told him and fished a coin from his poke and plunked it down. "Quiet little town you have here."

The bartender had turned to a shelf, and grunted.

"What do you do for excitement? Watch the grass grow?"

"Haven't heard that one before," the bartender said.

"Had much Indian trouble hereabouts?" Fargo wondered. The Cheyenne had been acting up recently. They'd had their fill of the white invasion and were raiding homesteads and attacking stagecoaches.

"Doesn't everybody?" was the barman's response.

"I'm not asking everybody," Fargo said. "I'm asking you."

The bartender selected a glass from a pile next to a dirty cloth and picked up the dirty cloth and wiped it. "Our problem ain't Injuns. It's outlaws. They've hit three farms in the past couple of months and struck the Overland stage and got away with the money box." He set the glass on the bar and turned and chose a bottle.

Fargo picked up the glass. "You call this clean?" He wasn't fussy but there was . . . something . . . crusted a quarter-inch thick on the bottom, and a few brown smudges besides.

"I just wiped it. You saw me."

"It would be cleaner if I wiped it with my ass."

"Here now," the barkeep said indignantly. "You're not funny."

"Do you see me laughing?"

The man looked at Fargo and opened his mouth to say something but seemed to think better of it and held out his hand. "Give it to me. I'll wash it."

Fargo watched him dip it in a bucket of dirty water and then dry it with the dirty cloth. "You're something," he said.

"How's that again?"

"Forget the glass. I'll buy a bottle. One that hasn't been opened."

"First you want a clean glass and now you want a bottle," the bartender grumbled. "I wish you'd make up your mind."

"I just did."

Fargo's tone caused the barman to stiffen. "I don't want no trouble. I'm just doing my job."

"A goat could do it better."

Turning to a shelf lined with bottles, the barkeep muttered, "You have no call to insult me."

"The bottle," Fargo said. "This year."

"Damn, you are prickly."

Fargo snatched the bottle and opened it himself and tilted it to his mouth. The burning sensation brought a welcome warmth and he could feel himself relax.

"Happy now?"

Just then the batwings creaked and in came half a dozen cowboys. Smiling and joshing one another, they strolled to the bar.

One of them bumped Fargo with his shoulder and went on talking to his pard. About to take a swallow, Fargo felt his arm jostled a second time and whiskey spilled onto his chin.

". . . heard that calf when we branded it," the cow nurse was saying. "It screamed just like a female, I swear."

"Peckerwood," Fargo said, and jabbed the puncher with his elbow so hard, it rocked the cowboy onto his bootheels.

"What the hell was that for?" the cowboy demanded, growing red in the face.

"You know damn well." Fargo sleeved his chin with his buckskins. "Bump me again and I'll lay you out."

"I'd like to see you try."

Fargo should have let it go. That's what anyone with a lick of common sense would do. But the cowpoke's smug smirk was like a slap to the face. Then there was the unwritten law that you never, ever jostled a man taking a drink. "I believe I will," he said, and swung.

No other series packs this much heat!

THE TRAILSMAN

Follow the trail of Penguin's Action Westerns at
penguin.com/actionwesterns

NOW AVAILABLE IN PAPERBACK

THE LAST OUTLAWS
The Lives and Legends of Butch Cassidy and the Sundance Kid

by Thom Hatch

Butch Cassidy and the Sundance Kid are two of the most celebrated figures of American lore. As leaders of the Wild Bunch, also known as the Hole-in-the-Wall Gang, they planned and executed the most daring bank and train robberies of the day, with an uprecedented professionalism.

The Last Outlaws brilliantly brings to life these thrilling, larger-than-life personalities like never before, placing the legend of Butch and Sundance in the context of a changing—and shrinking—American West, as the rise of 20th century technology brought an end to a remarkable era. Drawing on a wealth of fresh research, Thom Hatch pushes aside the myth and offers up a compelling, fresh look at these icons of the Wild West.

Available wherever books are sold or at penguin.com

National bestselling author

RALPH COMPTON

SHADOW OF THE GUN
DEATH OF A BAD MAN
RIDE THE HARD TRAIL
BLOOD ON THE GALLOWS
THE CONVICT TRAIL
RAWHIDE FLAT
THE BORDER EMPIRE
THE MAN FROM NOWHERE
SIXGUNS AND DOUBLE EAGLES
BOUNTY HUNTER
FATAL JUSTICE
STRYKER'S REVENGE
DEATH OF A HANGMAN
NORTH TO THE SALT FORK
DEATH RIDES A CHESTNUT MARE
RUSTED TIN
THE BURNING RANGE
WHISKEY RIVER
THE LAST MANHUNT
THE AMARILLO TRAIL
SKELETON LODE
STRANGER FROM ABILENE
THE SHADOW OF A NOOSE
THE GHOST OF APACHE CREEK
RIDERS OF JUDGMENT
SLAUGHTER CANYON
DEAD MAN'S RANCH
ONE MAN'S FIRE
THE OMAHA TRAIL
DOWN ON GILA RIVER
BRIMSTONE TRAIL
STRAIGHT SHOOTER
THE HUNTED
HARD RIDE TO WICHITA
TUCKER'S RECKONING

"A writer in the tradition of Louis L'Amour and Zane Grey!" —*Huntsville Times*

Available wherever books are sold or at
penguin.com   S543

GRITTY WESTERN ACTION FROM

USA TODAY BESTSELLING AUTHOR
RALPH COTTON

Available wherever books are sold or at
penguin.com